ROAD OF SOULS
Copyright © MCMLXXVII by P. J. Thorndyke Productions. All Rights Reserved.
All characters and events in this film are fictitious. Any similarity
to actual persons living or dead is purely coincidental.

Road of Souls
By P. J. Thorndyke

https://pjthorndyke.wordpress.com/

Chapter 1

Southern California, July 1977

The Winnebago glided along as Rick and Diane made their way up the Ortega Highway, following the old Indian trail through the Santa Ana Mountains. There were no other vehicles on the road and the sluggishly sinking sun shone off the mountains, stretching the shadows, making all seem syrupy and dreamlike.

Rick kept his eyes on the distant heat lines rising from the two-lane highway as he held the steering wheel firmly, almost trancelike in his determination not to make any mistakes. He was tired and a slip in concentration now could be deadly.

"Dangerous stretch of highway", the man at the gas station in Lake Elsinore had said. "Folks get killed several times a year between here and Orange County. Motorcyclists, mostly. Out to prove something. Keep your wits about you and your speed down and you'll be fine."

Yeah, motorcyclists, thought Rick. Ninety percent of accidents are caused by other people. He didn't know if he had read that somewhere, but it sounded about right. Other assholes on the road, that was the real danger. You never knew who you might run into.

He took each hairpin turn nice and slow, easing the bulk of the camper through the treacherous series of twists and turns as they rose higher and higher. Lake Elsinore was a flat mirror below them, sometimes on their left, sometimes on their right as they wound their way up through the mountains. *No rush. If we don't make San Juan Capistrano by nightfall, then there are plenty of good camping spots on this stretch of highway.* It was already late. The sun was setting, turning the mountains to golden fire. And he wanted a drink.

"There's a campground not far after the turnoff for Ortega Falls," Diane said, almost reading his mind as she examined the folding map.

"That'll do just fine," said Rick, briefly taking his eye off the road to glance at the black and white clock on the dash slowly ticking off the minutes. It was nearly six. Time to clock off and enjoy a cold one. This *was* their summer vacation. Despite everything.

Hell. Last fall they had taken the plunge and put several grand down on a Winnebago Chieftain and this was their maiden voyage in it; to look for Diane's kooky little sister who had gone swanning off to California and gotten herself lost. Diane was worried sick about her, and Rick guessed he would be too if it was anybody else. But Christine had always been a wild child. Her taste in boyfriends had been lousy when she was a teenager and he doubted if it had improved since she moved out of their parents' house two years ago.

She had been living with two other girls in some pad in Greenwich Village where she spent her nights (and every paycheck from her job as a librarian's assistant) on the Manhattan disco scene. God knew who she had run into in those dives. Her housemates said she had recently met a guy she seemed besotted with but neither of them had clapped eyes on him.

She had been going steady with him for a while and then suddenly announced that he was taking her to California. She had packed in her job and flew the coop with this guy, sending occasional postcards to Diane and their parents from Laguna Beach and Santa Ana. She sometimes called Diana, telling her what a terrific time she was having but being decidedly cryptic about where she was and who she was with. And then – *poof!* Radio silence. No more postcards or calls and none of the telephone numbers she had given Diane yielded any fruit. Nobody seemed to know where Christine was.

The police wouldn't do anything and, against Rick's pleas to the contrary, Diane had hired a private detective out of his office in Los Angeles. He had rooted around and kept them updated with weekly phone calls. Apparently, Christine had gotten involved with some shady types who were in some sort of cult or something. *Typical California.* And then the detective had stopped checking in too. More phone calls to L.A. revealed that he had blown his brains out in a sleazy motel room.

That had done it for Diane. She had been worried before but now she was convinced that something sinister had happened to Christine. The detective had probably uncovered too much and had been murdered, at least that was her theory on it. As far as Rick was concerned, Christine was probably strung out in some dope pad with whatever loser she had shacked up with, thinking of no one but herself as usual. And the private detective undoubtedly had his own problems that had caused him to take his own life. These PIs must see some godawful things in their line of work that were bound to take their toll on a man's sanity. Coincidence, that was all. Nothing sinister. *But try telling Diane that ...*

Now they had to spend their summer vacation driving across the country to find someone who probably didn't want to be found and surely wouldn't show any gratitude.

"You doing OK?" Diane asked, giving him that concerned look he hated.

"Yeah, just a little tense," he replied, realizing that he had one of his deep frowns on. "This highway is no joke."

They passed the Lookout Roadhouse on Lake Elsinore Vista Point and began winding their way south-west through the mountains. There was more shade here as the live oaks and tall pines grew thick on both sides of the highway.

Rick saw the Dodge van in his wingmirror coming up fast on their ass. It swerved into the other lane to get a peek at the bend ahead to see if the coast was clear.

"Don't try it, pal," Rick muttered.

But the driver of the van *was* trying it. Rick watched, appalled, as the vehicle swung out into the road on a blind curve and began to speed up with the intent of overtaking. Rick braked gently, to give the madman a chance to swoop in front of him if another vehicle suddenly appeared around the bend.

The van was a custom job; midnight blue with a wizard surrounded by crackling lightning painted on the side. Its windows were open and, as it passed, heavy metal music could be heard from inside. Wisps of smoke billowed out along with the tortured guitar riff and Rick could see three figures seated in the front; kids with long hair. Could be boys or girls (who could tell these days?). A beer can was tossed out the window and it bounced off the Winnebago's windshield, leaving a spatter of foamy residue.

Rick swore and slammed on the brakes.

"Jesus!" Diane complained as she nearly slid out of her seat.

"Crazy bastards!" said Rick, switching on the windshield wipers to clear his view of the road ahead. He palmed the horn angrily but the van was way up ahead now, vanishing around the curve of the mountain, a middle finger at the end of an arm thrust out from the driver's window as a parting gift.

"Goddamn kids!" said Rick, feeling his blood boil. "They think they're gonna live forever. Well, let 'em kill themselves I say, but leave the rest of us out of it!"

"They were just horsing around," said Diane.

"Don't you start defending them, Diane! There's no excusing that kind of behavior!"

"I know, I know. I wasn't defending them. Just don't let them distract you. They've gone now."

Rick exhaled slowly, trying to release some of the pent-up tension. He was still annoyed but, as Diane had said, they were gone now.

They had passed the highest peak now and the road became less twisty as it descended southeastwards towards El Cariso. Bean fields and orange groves grew on either side of the highway and the sheer drops had been replaced by rolling grasslands burnt brown by the sun. It was a pleasant evening and Rick let himself sink into it a little, his mind on that first cold can of Miller's straight from the refrigerator that he would enjoy once they had pulled up for the night.

He was about to ask Diane if they were near that campground yet when they passed a layby and the midnight blue van roared out of it, its wheels kicking up dust as it fishtailed its way into the Winnebago's wake.

"Those bastards ..." Rick mumbled, glancing into his wingmirror. "They've been waiting for us."

"Is it the same van?" Diane asked.

"You bet."

The van gave a series of angry blasts on its horn as it closed in on the camper, tailgating it.

"Jesus, what's their problem?" Rick said.

"Honey, I'm scared," said Diane.

"They're just kids out for kicks," said Rick, realizing that the roles had reversed and now it was him making excuses instead of Diane.

"What if they're not?"

Rick said nothing. He knew what Diane was thinking because he was thinking the same thing. The headlines of the paper they had seen on the newsstand in Lake Elsinore described the recent grisly finding in an orange grove in that area; of a young waitress who had been stabbed to death and buried in a shallow grave. Her heart had been removed. Police were considering a link to the gruesome murder of another woman whose headless body had been found in the restroom of a gas station in Santa Ana. The heart of that girl had also been cut out. There was talk of some satanic cult operating in the area which inevitably had Diane on high alert, increasing her concern for her sister's welfare. Rick thought it was probably just some nut with a hard-on for butchery.

But what if...

But what if it really was the work of some Manson-type hippie freaks? Three kids who travelled up and down this highway in a custom painted van looking for weary travelers to murder? They hadn't passed a single vehicle in over twenty minutes. This stretch of highway was desolate and the shadows in the orange groves on either side seemed to grow deeper by the second.

He tried to dispel those thoughts. Kids out for kicks, that's all it was.

The van cruised alongside just as it had done before. Its windows were rolled up now and they were tinted, obscuring the kids' faces.

With a sudden lurch, the van veered towards the Winnebago. Rick yanked on the steering wheel and the right tires of the camper rumbled onto the hard earth.

"Oh, my God!" Diane cried. "Be careful!"

"If they scratch this paintjob, I'll ...!" Rick began.

The van had moved away and was giving them some room. Rick wasn't fooled but he didn't want any scratches from the bushes and tree branches that were whipping by on his right so he edged both sets of tires back onto the blacktop. The van swooped in again.

"Oh, you think this is funny, huh?" said Rick, veering onto the verge again.

The thought of pulling over crossed his mind but he quickly dismissed it. They were out in the middle of nowhere and there was no telling what these doped-up screwballs might be capable of.

The kids seemed to have got their kicks for the time being and they slowed down and steered back into the lane behind them. Rick slowly pressed down on the gas pedal to increase the distance between the two vehicles. The van hung back and began to grow distant.

"Think they've given up?" Diane asked as the van vanished behind a bend.

"I hope to God they have. How far to that campground?"

"Just a couple of miles."

The van seemed to come out of nowhere. Rick's tired eyes had been focused on the road ahead and Diane had her eyes on the map so neither of them had seen it approaching in their wingmirrors. It slammed into their rear fender, sending a jolt through the camper. Diane screamed as the large vehicle began to weave across the road. Rick gripped the steering wheel, his fists like vices as he struggled to maintain control. The Winnebago had barely ceased swerving when the van rammed it again.

Christ, they're really trying to kill us! Rick thought, the horror of the situation fully setting in now. He eased his foot on the brake pedal and fought for traction on the road. The yellow centerline wavered about like a lethal snake beneath the camper's chassis as its wheels drifted left and right.

"Rick, lookout!" Diane cried, pointing at the pickup truck that was fast approaching in the other lane.

The pickup's horn blared and Rick gritted his teeth, willing the camper to drift back into the righthand lane in time.

They just made it and the red flash of the pickup zipped passed the left wingmirror with inches to spare. It had slammed on its brakes and its tires were screeching in protest as it too lost control. Rick gazed at the scene in his wingmirror in horror as the pickup nearly ploughed into the blue van head on. The van veered off the road just in time and both vehicles were enveloped in swirling dust clouds as they came to a standstill.

"Shouldn't we stop?" Diane said.

"Like hell! I just hope that old boy has a shotgun in his pickup and gives those kids a hide full of pellets! Jesus, I'm shaking."

His fists seemed unable to release their death-grip on the steering wheel. His heart hammered in his chest and he wanted that beer now more than ever. If his stomach could hold it.

"Look, there's a diner," said Diane. "Want to pull over for a moment? Maybe they have a phone. We should call the cops."

"Damned straight."

The diner was more of a roadhouse and was clearly popular with motorcyclists judging by the number of hogs lined up outside. There were a few other vehicles too; station wagons and pickups. Plenty of people. That was good. Civilization at last.

They rumbled into the parking lot and Rick prized his hands from the wheel so he could fling open the door and spill out of his seat. He stood with his hands on his knees for a moment, willing his body to stop shaking.

"Honey?" Diane asked, coming around to his side. "Are you gonna throw up?"

"Nah. Just need a moment is all."

He straightened and took a deep lungful of the warm evening air scented with pines and the smell of the cooling desert hills. Then he went around the back of the Winnebago to take a look at the damage.

It wasn't too bad, considering. The aluminum fender was dented pretty good and the ladder looked like it had taken a knock but the spare wheel seemed to be unscathed. That didn't make Rick feel any happier about the whole thing, though.

"Bastards! We lug this brand-new camper across the country without a scratch only for some local psychos to beat the hell out of it just as we reach our destination."

"We're alive," said Diane. "Let's just be thankful for that."

They went indoors and found the place comfortably busy. Rick headed for the restroom to freshen up while Diane enquired about the use of a telephone. He splashed his face with cold water from the faucet and gazed at his pallid reflection in the mirror. *Jesus*. He *was* still alive. Just about. He dried himself off with paper towels and left the restroom.

Men were sitting at the bar swilling beer from bottles and frosted tankards. By God, he was going to have one right now. His nerves needed it. They were near the campground anyway. The day was over and what a bastard of a day it had been.

"The phone is in the other room," said Diane, jerking her thumb in the direction of an archway showing a pair of bikers playing a round of pool under the low-hanging light. "Let's call the cops and tell them what happened."

"Sure," said Rick. He began fishing around in his pocket for a quarter. Then, he froze, his eyes fixed on the big window that looked out onto the parked bikes and cars. The blue van was cruising into the parking lot, the painted wizard on its side streaked with dust.

"Son of a bitch," he muttered.

"Rick?" said Diane. She followed his gaze and then let out a gasp.

Rick started for the door, his blood boiling once more. All thoughts of calling the police or ordering a beer had vanished from his mind. All he could think of was letting these scumbags have it right there in the parking lot. They weren't in the middle of nowhere now. *Let's see how brave they are with all these witnesses!*

"Rick, wait!" Diane pleaded as she tugged on his arm. "Let's call the police!"

He shook her off and flung open the door to the diner, taking big strides towards the blue van. Three teenagers had clambered out of it, two boys and girl, all straggly hair and ripped denim. The two boys had band t-shirts on; one was Black Sabbath and the other was those painted Kiss freaks.

Rick didn't know which of them had been the driver and he didn't care. He grabbed the one with the Kiss t-shirt and slammed him against the side of the van.

"Listen to me, you little punk!" he roared into the kid's face. "You psychos nearly killed us back there. Is there something wrong with your fucking heads?"

"Hey, man!" the kid complained, trying to wriggle out of Rick's grip. "Get your hands off me!"

Rick slammed him against the van again. The kid's two buddies were uselessly letting him take it and were watching Rick with scowls on their faces.

"I'm warning you, scumbag!" Rick hissed at his captive. "If we have any more trouble from you on the road, I'll kill you! I swear to God, I'll run that piece of shit van off the road and kill all three of you!"

"Rick, for God's sake!" Diane said behind him.

Rick released the kid and took a step back, his chest heaving. He had seen red for a while there, but he thought his message had gotten across. As he walked away from the three kids, the one he had roughed up yelled; "Big mistake, man! You're gonna regret fucking with us!"

"I'm quakin' in my shoes!" Rick called back. He expected some sort of retort, but the three kids just stood there, their faces burning with silent anger.

A crowd of spectators had gathered in the parking lot, drawn from their meals and drinks by the dust-up. They gazed at Rick like he was an exotic plant. He ignored them as he made his way back inside.

"What the hell were you thinking?" Diane said, accompanying him through the door. "They could have killed you."

"Uh-uh, Honey. Just dumb kids out for kicks, just as I thought. You saw how they crumpled when I confronted them? Bunch of cowards! But I showed them who's boss. I suspect we won't have any more trouble from them. Look, see? They're leaving!"

The three teenagers had piled back into the blue van and it roared out of the parking lot and back onto the highway.

"I guess I put them off their milkshakes!"

"I don't think it's funny, Rick," said Diane disapprovingly. "We don't know what those kids are capable of."

"Relax. They're gone for good. Now, I don't know about you, but I'm having a beer."

"What about calling the cops?"

"Forget it. The cops won't do anything. Besides, I think I scared them enough that they won't try anymore funny stuff."

People began to file back into the restaurant and Rick ordered his beer. And by God, it was good.

Chapter 2

It was dark by the time they rolled into the campground. It was a shady little spot dotted with picnic benches beneath splayed oaks that partly shielded the starry sky. A couple of other campers were parked up, their interior lights on and the smell of barbecued meat drifting on the air, but other than that, they more or less had the place to themselves.

Diane was still sore at Rick whose mood had vastly improved after guzzling a frosted mug of Coors at the roadhouse. Despite the recent attempt on their lives, he was actually whistling as he set up the camping chairs and the folding table. Diane suspected that he was immensely pleased with himself for teaching those kids a lesson. It was amazing what roughing up a scrawny teenager could do for a man's spirits, she thought.

After dinner, while Rick sat out and smoked and gazed at the stars with a bottle of bourbon on the camping table next to him, Diane dragged out her box file and sat at the Formica table in the camper's dinette. This had become her nightly ritual. Every evening, after dinner, she would go through all the notes she had made, and the postcards Christine had sent her, analyzing them for any clues as to what her little sister had gotten herself into and where she might have gone. She had made notes on her conversations with private detective Ed Milton and, during their journey across the country from New York to California, she had been able to form a rudimentary timeline of events.

In February of that year, Christine had upped sticks and moved to Santa Ana, California with her boyfriend. Nobody knew who this guy was, not even his name. Christine's housemates had never seen him but said she had met him in a disco that January. On February 27th,

Christine had called Diane from a Santa Ana gas station and told her that she would be staying in California for a while. Diane had freaked out a little at her sister's impetuousness, but Christine had waved her worries aside, telling her that she wasn't a kid anymore and that it was time for her to strike out on her own and experience the world.

The following week Diane received a postcard from Laguna Beach that was almost cliché in its mundane brevity. It spoke of a swell time and listed a brief itinerary of things Christine had seen and done; ridden the rollercoaster at Knott's Berry Farm, gone fishing at Crystal Cove and explored the caves at Dana Point. There was something very off about the postcard. The sterile list of things to see and do in Orange County didn't sound like Christine at all. It was almost as if she was imitating somebody else. Or perhaps somebody else had written it. Diane had immediately called her parents and they confirmed that they had received an almost identical card. They agreed that something seemed way off.

A week of worrying went by and then Diane received a call from Christine.

"Hey," she had said. "It's me."

"Christine? Where are you? Are you all right?"

"I'm fine. I'm in California staying with some friends. I'm having a great time."

"Have you called Mom and Dad?"

"No. Just tell them I'm OK, huh?"

"Why can't you tell them yourself? They're worried sick!"

"They wouldn't understand. I'd get the usual grilling about who I'm with and what I'm doing with my life. They'd want me to come home. I just can't deal with all that right now. I called you because I knew you'd understand."

"Understand what?"

"That it's my life and I'll do what I want with it. If I want to head out to California then that's my business."

"Who are these friends you're with?"

"Jesus, don't you start, Diane."

"I just want to know that you're safe."

"They're super people and I'm fine."

"You still with that boy you headed out with?"

"Yeah. They're his friends. They have a pad by the beach, it's really terrific. I wish you could see it. I ... I miss you."

There was something there in her voice that set off alarm bells in Diane's head. Christine seemed *vulnerable*, like she needed her big sister. That's why she had called.

"Is there something you're not telling me, Christine?"

"What do you mean?"

"Is somebody there listening?"

"No."

"You can tell me anything, you know that, right?"

"Sure. Look, I have to go."

"Wait, where can I reach you? Can you give me a number?"

"Um, wait. OK. It's 996-7378. But I don't know how much longer I'll be here. We're all going up to O'Neill Park at the weekend."

Diane scribbled down the number on a pad along with O'Neill Park, wherever that was.

"Marty knows some people in the movie business who have a ranch house there. I might be able to get into the movies!"

"Marty?" Diane asked. "Is that your boyfriend's name?"

"Yeah."

"What's his last name?"

Christine sighed. "Don't get all Mom and Dad on me. I'm fine, really."

"OK but ..."

"I have to go. I love you, Sis."

"I love you too ..."

The line went dead.

Well, she was alive, that was something, Diane had told herself. But there was also something else. There was something Christine had wanted to tell her but hadn't dared. There was something she was frightened of. Diane could sense it in her voice. She had been way too serious for somebody who was apparently 'having a great time'.

There were no more phone calls or postcards for a month. Diane tried not to worry, tried to tell herself that Christine was a grown woman and had the right to a few adventures. She tried to tell herself that her misgivings were all in her head; natural worries of a big sister. Then, out of the blue, came the final phone call.

It was late at night. They had recently had a phone installed in the bedroom and Rick cursed something fierce to be woken by its shrill ringing at half past one in the morning.

"Christine?" Diane had said, rubbing some alertness into her eyes as she heard her little sister's voice on the other end of the phone.

"I just wanted to tell you that ... I love you ..."

"Christine?" Diane repeated. She sounded frightened, terrified even.

"And Mom and Dad ... tell them I love them OK?"

"Christine, what's going on?" Diane sat bolt upright in bed, her nerves kicked into high alert.

"I ... I just wanted to tell you that."

"Christine, you're scaring me!"

"I have to go now ..."

"No! Wait! Christine ..."

And the line had gone dead.

That panicked, late-night phone call on April 27th was the last anybody had heard from Christine. Naturally,

Diane had called the police but got nowhere. Christine was an adult and could do as she damn well pleased. Diane's insistence that something was horribly wrong, that her little sister was being threatened, held against her will or worse fell on deaf ears. There was no proof that a crime had been committed and therefore the police could do nothing.

That left the grubby and depressing world of private investigators.

Rick had been against it and Diane knew that he thought Christine was fine and all her worries were for naught. She'd turn up, he kept saying. No need to fork out handfuls of dough to a gumshoe who would probably take the money and run. But Diane wouldn't be deterred and Rick had eventually agreed, if only for his wife's sanity.

Diane had found Ed Milton's name in the Los Angeles phone directory and had struck up a friendly telephone relationship with him. She gave him what she had and he started asking around, quickly finding the pad Christine had crashed at in Laguna Beach. He grilled one of the girls who lived there and found out that Christine's boyfriend was part of some nutty bunch that was into drugs, meditation and occult shenanigans. They frequented witchy bookstores in Irvine and danced naked under the moon in O'Neill Park.

The girl was just an associate who had let them use her pad. She wasn't into it beyond smoking a little dope and hanging out with them. They had tried to get her to join them but she had told them it wasn't her scene. She claimed to be a Catholic, at least nominally, and all the occult hocus-pocus weirded her out a little. So, the gang had split and moved on. All she knew was that they were headed up to O'Neill Park to find more permanent digs.

"This occult stuff," Diane had asked Milton over the phone one night. "How serious is it? I mean, is it just a band of hippies?"

"Could be," said Milton.

"You don't sound certain."

"Because I'm not. Could just be hippie stuff. Or it could be something deeper than that. I remember what California was like ten years ago. There were a lot of weird folks running around, setting themselves up as gurus and forming cults. Still are if you know where to look. Most of them headed underground after the Manson killings made all that sort of thing a little unfashionable but Manson wasn't the half of it, believe me."

"*Is* my sister part of a cult?"

"Well, it could just be a small-time thing. These kids sound like drifters so I wouldn't think they're part of anything bigger. But this connection they seem to have to O'Neill Park concerns me somewhat. You said they knew people in the movie business with a ranch out there?"

"That's what Christine told me."

"The old 'I can make you a star, kid' line is a pretty worn one out here. Ninety-nine percent of the time it's just bullshit to get into a girl's panties. But that's my next lead. I'm heading up there tomorrow to see what's what. Somebody is bound to know something."

And then Ed Milton's line of enquiry had been cut frighteningly short when he had taken his own life a few days later. Diane didn't believe it was suicide. These private investigators were by nature a pathologically curious bunch and she couldn't believe one of them would kill themselves when they were in the middle of a case. Between cases, she might see it, when life was quiet and dull and all they did was drink and smoke and wait for the next case like Humphrey Bogart in one of those old movies. But not when the clues were piling up and the end of the case was in sight. No way. Something had happened to Ed Milton. Somebody had gotten to him and murdered him. He had found out too much and had been killed for it.

And now they were following in their footsteps. God help them. *And God help Christine, wherever she is.*

It was Milton's death that convinced her that Christine had not just fallen in with a bunch of harmless hippies. It had to be some sort of cult and a dangerous one at that. The newspapers they had seen at Lake Elsinore with their stories of corpses with their hearts removed for satanic rites had filled her with dread. Christine couldn't possibly be mixed up in something like that, surely?

Rick came in, banging the door to the camper a little louder than a sober man might.

"It's getting cold out!" he announced as he shoved the bottle of bourbon back in its cubbyhole behind Diane's head.

He was drinking more these days. It was noticeable.

"Any fresh clues, Sherlock?" Rick said, eyeing the stack of papers Diane had spread out on the Formica tabletop.

"No," she replied, massaging her temples. "I'm just going through it all before our appointment with Detective Garrett tomorrow."

"You really think that's our next move?" Rick asked as he collapsed into the seat opposite her and began unlacing his shoes.

"Yes. He's the man investigating Ed Milton's death."

"Ed Milton's *suicide*," Rick corrected her.

She said nothing while she packed up all the documents and began placing them back in the box file.

"You're really convinced there's some sort of connection between Milton's death and Christine's disappearance, don't you?"

"No, Rick, I'm not convinced," she said in a tired voice. "I just think it's a hell of a coincidence, that's all.

Our trip to the Orange County Sheriff's Office tomorrow might all be for nothing. Detective Garrett might not have anything for us at all. Or he might be able to provide some clue Milton uncovered before his death that he was never able to pass on to us. It might be the missing link and might even allow us to pick up where he left off."

"OK, honey, I know what this means to you." He held up his hands to show he meant no malice. "I just don't want you to be too disappointed if it's a big fat nothing. Now, I'm for bed. I'm beat!"

Diane was tired too and she went to brush her teeth while Rick crashed about in the sleeping compartment next door. When she emerged from the tiny bathroom cubicle, he was already tucked in and snoring softly. She sighed, slipped into her nightie and got into her own bed.

The Winnebago Chieftain D-27C had the rather un-romantic layout of two single beds separated by a nightstand. She supposed it was just as well. After all, why pretend? They hadn't made love in four months. What was the point? Six years of trying had resulted in three miscarriages and a series of depressing appointments with Dr. Preston who had done his best to let them down gently and ease them into the idea that having kids was unlikely.

She knew Rick didn't blame her, at least on a conscious level. He had actually told her that it wasn't her fault, as if that was any consolation to her. But she knew the news had hit him hard and deep down there must be some resentment, even if he wasn't aware of it himself. His temper had worsened in the past year, as had his drinking. She guessed he was struggling with it just as she was.

It was after they had both turned thirty that they decided to buy the Winnebago. All the money they had saved for their dream of starting a family was sitting in their bank account doing nothing. Why not use it on something they might enjoy? Rick had said. Get out of New York and see the country. Get some proper R&R. They deserved it.

Diane knew he was right, and the thought of owning a camper did appeal to her but once the down payment on the vehicle had been made, she felt as if she had abandoned something, betrayed something. *Given up* on someone. It was someone not yet born (*and never would be*) but all the same, she felt guilty. It was silly, she knew, but the purchase of the Winnebago seemed to finalize the awful news from Dr. Preston. As the Winnebago rumbled into their drive, shiny and new, Diane felt that her baby's replacement had arrived and with it their new lives. Now there was no going back. They would grow old together, her and Rick, and they would take this magnificent machine out on weekend trips and she would clean it and keep it nice and it would see them well into their retirement. This is what they would do instead of being parents. The dream would fade in time. Forget it. Move on. Go camping.

A sob welled in Diane's chest as she lay there in the dark listening to Rick snoring. She squeezed her eyes tight and forced it down. *Don't give in to it*, she told herself. This trip was about finding Christine. It wasn't about the state of their marriage or the soreness she felt when she let her mind dwell on the kids they would never have. *Find Christine.* That was her mission, and she did not have the luxury of allowing herself to be distracted from it.

CHAPTER 3

When Rick had been nine years old, he had gone missing. His mom had sent him to the store on the corner of their street in Yonkers to buy some washing detergent and he had not come back. She called a couple of Rick's friends to see if he had stopped by to play with them. Their mothers said he had not. Then, leaving Rick's little sister Karen in her highchair to continue splashing her oatmeal around, Rick's mother had quickly walked the distance to the store and back, hoping to run into Rick on the way. She didn't.

That was when the fear began to set in. She called her husband at work and told him that Rick was missing. He told her to calm down and that Rick was probably off playing marbles in some alley or shooting at tin cans with an air rifle and no, he couldn't possibly leave work to help look for him. He hung up and Rick's mother notified the police. They were about as interested as Rick's father had been and said more or less the same things he had. Kids turn up, they told her. But it did nothing to slow her mounting terror.

The evening approached and Rick's dad came home to find Rick's mother frantically clutching their baby daughter in one arm and the telephone in the other, pouring out her worst fears to a friend on the other line. Rick's dad didn't even take his coat off and went straight back out to look for Rick, muttering under his breath that the boy would have a hard time sitting down for a while after he had found him.

Rick's dad searched the streets until nightfall. Several concerned neighbors joined him. They searched every alley, every park and under every bridge until around midnight when it was decided that nothing more could be done for the time being. Rick's dad had reluctantly returned home to his distraught wife and they spent a sleepless night sitting by the phone.

The search continued at the break of dawn and the area was widened to include the old Croton Aqueduct path that cut through a densely wooded area below Untermeyer Park. This tangled, neglected area was a communal dumping ground roamed by the homeless derelicts who made their dwellings out of sight of the clapboard houses and picket fences of Northwest Yonkers. It was around noon when word began to filter back south that the boy had been found and he was alive.

It was an off-duty police officer helping out in the search who found Rick stumbling out of the grounds of Untermeyer Park. This sprawling garden estate populated by classical temples and pavilions had fallen into neglect since the death of its creator, Samuel Untermeyer, in 1940. Its statues of sphinxes and lions were black with age and its Indo-Persian garden pools had dried up leaving behind cracked mosaics partially obscured by dead leaves. From this wasteland of a dead dream, Rick had emerged, blinking in the sunlight.

He was immediately taken to the police station where, after being checked over by a doctor, he was released into the care of his tearful parents. He couldn't seem to remember anything of what had happened, only that he remembered walking to the store and then emerging from the old pump house in Untermeyer Park some five miles north. Everything in between was a blur. The only thing he could tell anybody was that he remembered holding the hand of a tall, gray man.

That had set some alarm bells ringing. Had the kid been abducted by a pervert? Carried off to the ruins of Untermeyer Park and ... *interfered* with? The doctor had found nothing medically wrong with the kid but clearly something traumatic enough had happened to him that his mind had blocked it out.

The cops rousted the homeless wretches who dwelt along the Croton Aqueduct path. They even paraded them before young Rick in the hopes that he might pick one of them out, but Rick didn't recognize any of them. The cops ruefully sent the bums on their way and shrugged their shoulders at the unsolved mystery. The kid seemed to be fine and, in any case, he was home now, safe and sound. All involved resigned themselves to the fact that if the kid couldn't remember anything, then nothing further could be done.

But the events of that night remained with Rick, lurking in the back of his memory like a tangled ball of yarn. He remembered nothing more as the years passed, only the cold, slippery feel of that tall gray man's hand in his and the sensation of *going* somewhere with him. It came to him in dreams like an old movie playing over and over in his head and, try as he might, he could remember no more of it. His subconscious chewed over the events of twenty-one years ago. The tall gray man. The cold, slippery hand. The cave.

Cave?

He had never dreamt of a cave before. But here he was, nine-years-old again, holding the gray man's hand, standing at the mouth of a cave.

It was dank and dark and smelled of dead things. He could hear dogs barking and whining in the recesses of the blackness. He was scared. He wanted to look up at the gray man's face but he didn't dare. He willed himself to look, desperate to solve the mystery of his childhood but his neck muscles were frozen with fear.

The gray man led him deeper into the cave. The howling of the dogs grew louder and there was another noise too; a low, monotonous chanting. All around him was blackness. He couldn't even see the gray man next to him, but he could feel his hand in his. The chanting increased in tempo and volume, drowning out the sound of the dogs. It was all around him. Many people were there but he couldn't see them. The gray man had let go of his hand now and he was adrift in the blackness. He looked this way and that, trying to pick out something for his eyes to focus on. Then, his eyes caught two shiny red objects some distance from him. He squinted, trying to figure out what they were. The red pinpricks grew in intensity and became larger. Rick got the sensation of something approaching and he suddenly screamed as he recognized the objects for what they were. Eyes! Red, glowing eyes!

He awoke to the horrible sensation that whatever owned those eyes had him in its tangled grasp and was crushing the life out of him. He realized that he was tangled up in his sheet and the darkness around him was the interior of the Winnebago in the year 1977, not wherever the hell he had been that night in 1956.

He threw the blanket off him and let the sweat cool on his skin. The air was stuffy and hot. They had forgotten to open a window. Diane snored gently in her bunk, undisturbed by his thrashings, her own blanket pulled up to her chin How could she sleep like that in this heat?

A noise outside the camper startled him. A sort of scraping sound of metal on metal. He blinked in the darkness, wondering what the hell it could be. A racoon? A mountain lion?

There was a wrenching sound as of tortured metal that sent a gentle shake through the camper. Then he heard whispering. A stifled giggle.

I'll be goddamned, he thought. *That's no wildlife.* Somebody was fucking with the camper!

He got up as gently as he could so as not to alert whoever was outside to the fact that he was awake. He wanted to catch these bastards on the hop. It crossed his mind that it might be those same teenagers who had so spoilt their day come back to get their revenge. Well, if they had damaged the Winnebago in any way, he'd do some fucking damage to them.

Diane slept on as Rick crept out of the sleeping compartment and to the front of the vehicle. He took his bathrobe with him for he was dressed only in his briefs and wasn't about to confront anybody while half-naked. Silently unlatching the door, he stepped down onto the ground outside.

It was still pitch black and Rick realized he should have checked his watch which lay on the nightstand. He had no idea what time it was. The night air was scented with pine needles which carpeted the ground, making his footfalls next to inaudible as he circled the camper.

There was nobody about. He cursed. Damned kids must have heard him and hightailed it out of there. He looked the camper over to make sure nothing had been done to it and froze when he saw the open door to the storage locker on the right-hand side. It was a useful cubbyhole for things that were too bulky to fit inside the camper; a fire extinguisher, toolbox, the pump for the inflatable raft. Rick felt his blood boil as he inspected the damaged locker. The door had been jimmied and was so bent out of shape that it wouldn't even close now. Undoubtedly, that was the sound that had woken him. He looked inside to see if anything had been stolen. His toolkit was still there but he was too mad to think clearly about what else the locker had contained.

Those little bastards!

He spun around, hoping to catch sight of them running off. The camping ground was utterly still beneath the silent trees. He couldn't even see the other campers. All had their lights off and silence reigned like a dark blanket.

But no, it wasn't complete silence. He could hear *something*. Distant music. *Heavy metal.* It was muffled, as if from inside a vehicle but he could definitely hear it.

He walked away from the camper, following his ears. The music grew louder as he moved through the trees towards the road. He emerged onto the blacktop and looked up and down. There were no vehicles driving at this dead hour of the night but there was one parked in a layby on the other side of the road a little further along. It was a blue custom van with a wizard on its side.

Rick gritted his teeth. He knew it! Those bastard kids!

Pulling his bathrobe around himself as if it would give him a tad more dignity, he marched across the road towards the vehicle. By God, they had done it now! He'd do more than yell at them this time. And this time there were no witnesses!

The muffled music blared inside the car and there was nobody sitting up front. Probably in the back blasting their minds on reefer. He'd give them a good scare!

He went around to the back of the vehicle and grasped the handles of the double doors. With a jerk, he flung them both open at once.

Nobody screamed as he had hoped. There was no movement inside the back of the van, none at all. The electric light illuminated a scene of grotesque butchery. Blood coated all. It was sprayed up the interior walls, even across the ceiling. The shag carpet, if it had been any other color was a deep red now and the forms upon it took a while to register themselves in Rick's brain as he stood and stared on the scene of horror, utterly dumbfounded.

The tangle of limbs and torsos were so unnatural in their positioning that Rick wasn't sure he wasn't looking at some red arachnoid beast with multiple legs all jutting out at odd angles. As his eyes explored the gory heap, his mind tried to twist it all into some semblance of sanity. There were three bodies at least. It was difficult to tell because several of the limbs had been severed.

Once the monstrous shape had found some meaning in his mind, his stomach rose up into his chest cavity and he spun around and staggered for the bushes. He vomited heavily until dry heaves convulsed his sweating body and no more would come. Shaking, he straightened and faced the side of the van which stood silent with pregnant horror under the light of the moon. He didn't want to go and look again. *But I must!* He had to be sure that what he had seen was real.

Maybe it was a prank? Yeah, that was it! Those kids had lured him back here to prank him with a gallon of fake blood! In a minute they would all leap up and shout 'Boo!' and then they'd laugh and he'd laugh too just to show that there were no hard feelings. They'd make amends and go their own separate ways, all the bad blood (his stomach convulsed again at the word) all that bad *stuff* would be water under the bridge.

He returned to the rear of the van and peered in. The bodies still lay there, lifeless, almost artful in their stillness. The face of one of them – the girl – gaped at him from beneath the bent knee of one of her friends. Her eyes were open, as was her mouth; three shocked circles peering through a red mask.

There was something else amid the ruined bodies of the teenagers that was not organic. The haft of a large axe stood out at an angle, its wide iron head embedded in the face of one of the dead boys. It looked very much like the axe Rick owned and kept in the Winnebago's side locker for the chopping of firewood.

It couldn't be the same one, could it? He had been too jumped up to notice if it was missing when he came upon the broken-in locker. Why would somebody steal his axe and then murder three teenagers with it? The thought of a prank returned to him only this time it was the psychotic prank of a madman. Was somebody trying to frame him?

Or perhaps it wasn't his axe at all. He couldn't be sure. He would have to go back and check if it was missing from the locker. If it wasn't then he would call the police, notify them that a maniac was on the loose. But if his axe *was* missing ...

He hurried back across the road and through the trees towards the camping ground. The feverish heat that had radiated from his body minutes ago had dissipated now and he felt cold, either from fear or from being out in the night in just his bathrobe.

Once he reached the Winnebago, he checked the contents of the locker and reeled each item off his mental list of the things they had packed. The only thing that was missing was the large, double-handed axe.

His heart plummeting into black depths of despair, he crept back into the camper and sat down at the dinette. There could be no coincidence. The axe was his and now it was a murder weapon. He reached for the bottle of bourbon he kept in the cubbyhole by his head and fetched his glass from earlier that evening. He poured himself a generous measure and sat back down to mull over what he was going to do.

He had threatened those kids. In front of witnesses. They had all seen it. They had all heard him say that he would kill them if their paths crossed again. A figure of speech for God's sake! But he knew how prosecutors used people's words as weapons. And with his prints all over the murder weapon he would be finished in any courtroom. The jury wouldn't think twice before sending him down for triple homicide.

He took a deep gulp of bourbon and steeled his nerves for the decision his brain had just made. That axe had to be retrieved and disposed of. He briefly flirted with the idea of disposing of the van and the bodies too but that would be too difficult. The less he had to do with the crime scene the better. But the axe had to be removed, there was no getting around that. It was the only thing that tied him to the murder, except his heated words in the diner parking lot. That and the murder of those kids happening just over the road from where they had parked for the night. Boy, somebody had tried to fix him up good but there was nothing for it. He might just get away with those coincidences. *As long as he got rid of that axe.*

He finished off his drink and slowly stood up. The yellow marigolds Diane used for the washing up were jammed behind the faucet. Rick picked them up and stuffed them into the pocket of his bathrobe and set out once more.

He returned to the van, partly hoping that it had all been a bad dream and that the layby was empty. But it wasn't, and he pulled the marigolds out of his pocket and put them on with a diligent sense of grim purpose.

He stepped up into the van, wincing as his right shoe sank into the blood-soaked shag with an audible squelch. Scooping the flaps of his bath robe up around his middle so they wouldn't trail over the corpses, he made his way further into the van.

He seized the haft of the axe with one hand and gave it a half-hearted tug. It barely moved. Groaning, Rick knew that he was going to have to use both hands to get it loose. Letting the flaps of his bathrobe gently down, he gripped the haft with both hands and, marigolds squeaking, began to work it back and forth.

The head of the kid who had borne the axe's final chop rocked up and down as Rick miserably tried to free it. He thought the kid might be the one he had assaulted but he couldn't be sure as everything was coated with blood. He resigned himself to heaving upwards with all his might, lifting the kid's head off the shag carpet. The weight of the other bodies piled on top of the corpse prevented it from rising into a sitting position and, with a sudden and horrible sucking sound, the axe head came loose.

Rick nearly stumbled against the blood-spattered side of the van but regained his balance just in time. He stood swaying for a moment or two above the corpses, the heavy, blood-slicked axe in his hand.

Getting out of the van without getting blood on him was tricky but he felt that he had just about managed it. He would have to check his bathrobe thoroughly for any bloodstains and if there were any then he would have to dispose of it somehow and hope that Diane didn't start wondering where it went.

Christ, Diane! The thought of telling her what sort of a mess he was in hadn't even crossed his mind. He didn't think she'd actually believe that he'd killed those kids, even if he had threaten them, but he also didn't think he could bear for her to know about any of this. She already had so much on her mind looking for Christine and he didn't want to throw a wrench like this into the works. Besides, it was for her own protection. Say he did get picked up and linked to these murders. Diane would be able to say with all honesty that she had known nothing about it.

She was mercifully still asleep when he got back to the camper and began the next stage of his plan. He laid the axe down outside the camper and went in to fetch one of the blankets from a cupboard next to the bathroom. Going back out, he wrapped the axe up in the blanket and bound it with duct tape. This grisly parcel would have to be hidden somewhere onboard the camper until he found an opportunity to get rid of it in a spot where it would never be found. It terrified him to carry the murder weapon that could seal his doom with them but there was nowhere he could get rid of it on the campground. Better to find a river or a lake or something tomorrow.

And tomorrow was fast approaching. The sky in the east was already tinged with the flame of dawn. He stowed the bandaged murder weapon in the locker and sealed the broken door with duct tape. Then, he filled a bucket with water and sloshed off the soles of his shoes, leaving them outside to dry.

All that remained was to get back to bed and pretend that he had slept the night through. God knew, he wouldn't be sleeping any more that night.

CHAPTER 4

The evidence boxes were stark and under the hard fluorescent lighting of the interrogation room. Their contents were neatly organized and, in some cases, sealed in plastic bags. Clothes were folded. A gold watch, a safety razor and a nail clipper were bagged and tagged. A crumpled pack of cigarettes and a cheap plastic comb were treated with similar reverence.

It was all so sterile and seemed vaguely familiar to Diane who had spent enough of her career curating museum collections. She repressed a shudder at how the final days of somebody's life could be catalogued in a similar manner and it felt inappropriate for them to be rooting through it all. These were the personal effects of a man they had never met. Diane had spoken to him on the phone a few times but that was all. Now she was free to touch his possessions.

"Is this all that was found in his motel room?" she asked Detective Garrett.

"He was a light traveler," said the detective, a man in his mid-forties, greying and slightly thick in the middle. He had a tired hardness to him that suggested many years of dogged perseverance in a less than satisfying line of work. "A few items were found in his car including his snub revolver, but nothing that would help you find your sister."

Diane nodded as she gently sifted through the items in the boxes. "Was there any indication as to why he might have killed himself?"

Detective Garrett shrugged. "*Might* is the operative word in this case. It sure looks like he did it to himself. At least on the surface."

"But you think otherwise?"

"I'm not really at liberty to say what I think."

"What the hell does that mean?" said Rick. "You don't think Milton killed himself?"

"There's enough to support a theory that he didn't. But then, there is enough to convince most people that he did."

"What suggests that he didn't? Looks pretty clear to me that he blew his brains out."

Detective Garrett lit a cigarette and took a long drag while he considered his answer. "Firstly, who kills themselves with a 30-30 Marlin rifle when they have a perfectly good revolver? A rifle is a pretty unwieldy thing to turn on yourself. Forensic boys figure Milton sat on the edge of the bed, put the rifle butt on the floor and the other end in his mouth. That makes it hard to reach the trigger – not impossible – but hard. And like I said, a revolver was found in his car, so why didn't he use that? Secondly, there are aspects about the crime scene that don't quite add up."

"Like what?"

"Well, not to get too graphic but his head was damn near blown off. A round like that should've knocked him back onto the bed. The wall behind him was spattered with his brains but he was slumped forward, over the rifle. Maybe that's nothing. He could have bounced off the bed I guess."

"Or he could have been held in place," offered Diane. "Restrained while the gun barrel was put into his mouth."

"Yeah. But the funniest thing is the rifle itself. Milton owned it and we know he liked to go hunting when he wasn't on a case. But the rifle didn't have a single fingerprint on it."

"Almost as if somebody wiped it clean," said Diane.

"That's more or less what it suggested to me," Garrett replied. "Another thing; we found a spot of blood on the bathroom floor, below the sink. Now maybe Milton cut himself shaving. Or maybe ..."

"Maybe somebody knocked him out in the bath-room, then propped him up on the bed and blew his brains out with the rifle," Diane finished for him.

"Mmm-hmm. Could be. But like I said, this is all just theorizing. The sheriff thinks this is a suicide and that's what it's going to be written off as. It's worth more than my career to start causing trouble now especially when I'm not convinced it *wasn't* a suicide."

"Was there a note?" Rick asked.

Garrett shook his head. "Uh-uh. We've tried to re-construct Milton's actions on the day of his death and he seemed to have had a quiet one. He drove up to O'Neill Park in the morning and we don't know what he was do-ing there but a receipt in his pocket showed that he ate dinner at an In-N-Out in Irvine at around seven. Hardly what I would choose for my last meal. Then went back to his motel room apparently set on an early night. People in the neighboring rooms heard nothing from him until the gunshot at around eleven-thirty. If it wasn't a suicide, then the perps were mighty quiet about it."

"I feel like something's missing," said Diane as she continued to rifle through the mundane bits and pieces of a lonely life spent in motel rooms and cars. "Where are his notes? His evidence pertaining to the case he was in-vestigating. There's nothing here about my sister. Not a notebook, or a file or ..."

"The only bit of paper we found in the motel room was a photograph," Garrett interrupted. "It's in there, if you dig down."

Diane did so and pulled out a plastic baggie contain-ing a sun-bleached polaroid. As she inspected it, her eyes widened and her heartbeat quickened.

"This picture!" Diane said. "It's my sister!"

The polaroid had been taken outside, in some scrubby courtyard with the sun beating down strong. Christine was wearing pink hotpants and a white blouse and she stood alone in front of a broken wall. Her eyes looked left and the shadow of the person who had taken the picture was a dark blot in the bottom right corner. She wasn't smiling and her face wore the expression Diane recognized from childhood; one of vague uncertainty.

"We figured it was some broad he was seeing on the side, uh, begging your pardon," said Garrett. "Don't know where he got it or who gave it to him but if that's your sister then perhaps he was closer to finding her than you thought."

"Was there nothing else about Mr. Milton's investigation?" Rick asked. "Had he called anybody from the motel?"

"Yes, as a matter of fact. One number. We checked it out and it belongs to some smut peddler in L.A."

"Is he somehow connected to Christine's disappearance?"

"Not that we could figure. But we're investigating a suicide here, not a missing person."

"Right," said Rick coldly. "I forgot you weren't interested in finding her."

Garrett shrugged. "I could give you all the guff on how grown adults have the right to disappear if they want to, but I guess you've had all that before."

"We have," Diane said slowly. "Can I have this photograph?"

Garrett sucked his teeth. "This all has to go back to Ed Milton's agency. There's a fella coming to pick it up tomorrow. The case is closed and it's not evidence, but I still can't let you have any of it. I only agreed to let you look if it might help you find your sister."

"But what use would Milton's agency have for a picture of my sister?" Diane said. "We were his clients, after all and he would have eventually passed this on to us."

Garrett scratched his chin, undecided.

"Please, Detective," Diane pleaded. "I just want to find my sister. Pick up where Milton left off. This picture is our only lead."

"Well," said Garrett at last, "I guess nobody would miss it. And you were the late Ed Milton's clients after all. Sure, go ahead."

"Thank you."

They left the Orange County Sheriff's Department and walked back out into the hot sunshine. Diane clutched the polaroid of Christine to her breast protectively.

"Not too disheartened?" Rick asked her tentatively.

"Not at all," she replied. "This is the first sign of Christine we've had since I last spoke to her."

"Well, what now?" Rick said as they walked over to the Winnebago that sat cooking on the asphalt of the parking lot.

"Now we find out what interest this 'smut peddler' had for Milton. And what connection he had to Christine. I hope to God this wasn't the movie business connection she was talking about."

Rick glanced distastefully at the paper in his hand where he had jotted down the number Milton had called from his motel room.

"Ugh!" said Diane. "It all sounds so sordid and I can't imagine Christine getting involved in that sort of thing. But we must follow the trail, no matter how dark it gets or how awful its conclusion."

They found someplace to eat lunch and later Rick stepped into a phone booth to call the number he had jotted down. After a brief conversation with the character on the other end of the line, he established that the number belonged to a dirty bookstore in East Hollywood.

"Somehow I knew our search would lead us into L.A.," Rick said as he hung up the phone, his voice filled with the wary skepticism New Yorkers tended to have for Los Angeles.

"No matter where the trail goes, remember?" Diane said.

Rick grunted by way of voicing his disgust and they got back into the camper and headed northwest.

While Rick drove, Diane gazed at the polaroid of Christine, analyzing every inch of it, trying to find any clues as to where it was taken and what was going on in the picture. To anybody else it might look like a vacation picture snapped at some historic site in the Californian hills. But to Diane, who knew Christine, there was something off about it. Christine's expression for one thing didn't seem natural. She had known her sister long enough to tell when she was faking happiness. The expression in the photo matched the one used by the thirteen-year-old-girl at the dinner table who silently pleaded with her big sister not to tell Mom and Dad that she had snuck out the night before. It was the same half-smile she would perfect at the age of eighteen when she tried to pretend not to care that another relationship had gone down in flames while Diane could see that deep down her heart had been broken once again.

Who has you, Christine? she mused. *What are they doing to you?*

The shadow in the bottom corner loomed like a specter. Was this the elusive Marty the boyfriend? Why had he taken this picture and how had Ed Milton got hold of it? There were so many questions that Diane felt overwhelmed by the task of knowing which to ask first.

They rolled into L.A. and parked outside a liquor store and a small supermarket. After eating dinner at a hamburger stand to fortify themselves, they ventured into the seamy world of Hollywood Boulevard's early evening.

The sun set over the hills and stretched the shadows long down the warm asphalt. The Walk of Fame had petered out several blocks west. There were no terrazzo and brass stars studding these sidewalks, only dried circles of gum and squashed cigarette stubs. Some street walkers were out, leaning into car windows and hanging outside stores in pairs, all tight tops and hotpants. It alarmed Diane to see how closely their dress resembled what Christine was wearing in the polaroid. Was this the kind of life she had fallen into? Ed Milton had said she had joined a cult but all this was the sad and tired sex scene found in Times Square given a West Coast makeover. The weather was hotter than New York and there were palm trees, but it was all so depressing in its mundanity.

The establishment they were looking for was squished between a laundromat and an adult movie theatre. Its glowing purple sign described itself as a 'love boutique' and its dark interior was mostly screened by yellow cards in the windows advertising 'gadgets', 'porno films' and 'books & mags'. An inflatable doll propped up beneath a red light seemed shocked to be there.

"I'll go in," Rick said. "It wouldn't be proper for you ..."

"Thanks for the gentleman act, Rick," Diane said. "But I want to speak to this man myself."

Rick sighed as he pushed the glass door open and they went inside.

It was a dim, pokey place, all deep shadows and brilliant highlights that illuminated the book racks and display cases. One wall consisted of magazines with titles like 'Stud Shock' and 'Young and Very Hung'. Book racks and spinning displays catered to the more literary-minded customer but their covers were of a similar nature.

The proprietor stood behind a glass counter that contained various fleshy objects. He was a small man with shaggy hair and an attempt at a handlebar moustache. The only other person in the store was a middle-aged man who was perusing the magazine racks. A furtive glance at Diane made him blush and scurry for the door.

"We don't get too many lady-folks in here," the proprietor said, a smirk stretching the sides of his handlebar tash. "But that's OK. We ain't prejudiced. Everybody has their kinks and all are welcome here."

"Are you the owner?" Rick asked him.

"Owner? No. I just work here, man."

"But you more or less run the place, right?"

"That's me."

"My wife and I would like to ask you some questions."

"Wife?" His grin widened. "You brought your old lady to a sex store? I dig it, man."

"Did you ever speak with a Mr. Ed Milton?" Rick asked.

The man shook his head. "Never heard the name."

"He was a private detective. He called this store on the night of June 19th. Was it you he spoke to?"

The man straightened, a sudden nervousness banishing his expression of mild amusement. "Who are you people?" he asked.

"Relax," Rick told him. "We're just looking for my wife's little sister. We hired Milton and he seems to have called you before he died."

"Died? That guy's dead?"

"So you do remember him!"

"No! I mean, yeah, OK. I spoke to him. What happened?" There seemed to be a real fear in his eyes now. Almost as if he knew what Rick was about to say and was dreading it.

"He committed suicide."

"Supposedly," Diane added.

"Jesus! Are you saying he might have been snuffed?"

"It's a possibility," said Rick.

"What did Ed Milton call you about?" Diane said. "We only want to find my sister. Was it something to do with her?"

"I don't know!" the man said. "I don't know your sister!"

"Look at this picture please," said Diane as she slid the polaroid across the glass countertop towards him. "Have you ever seen her?"

He glanced at the picture. "No, I don't know her. That your sister? I never seen her. I never seen those movies, I just put this detective of yours in touch with the right people."

"What movies?" Rick said, leaning over the counter.

The man practically cowered in Rick's shadow. "Wait a minute," he said.

He sidled out from behind the counter and went over to the door. For a moment, Diane was worried that he was going to try and make a run for it, and she nearly cried out for Rick to stop him but the man turned the 'closed' sign over and locked the door. "Look," he said, returning to them. "I could really get in trouble for telling you anything and if that detective got offed then these guys are as serious as I think they are."

"Just tell us about these films," said Diane. "Tell us what you told Milton and it'll stay between us."

"OK," the man said with a deep sigh. "This private detective comes to me one day out of the blue and starts asking about films made by a director called Muscado. He's trying to track down one of the stars of these movies but as soon as he told me the director's name, I knew I had bad news for him."

"How do you mean?" Diane asked, her heart skipping a beat.

"You ever heard of snuff films?" His raised eyebrow was conspiratorial.

"No, I haven't," Diane replied. "What are they?"

"Well, there's all kinds of kicks for all kinds of folks. Some people like standard smut. Some like whips and chains. You still with me?"

"Yes," said Diane.

"And some, well, *some* go in for a more illicit kind of thrill. The kind that has to be kept secret. The kind that people like myself won't touch. Snuff is in that ballpark. The star of a snuff movie only stars in one movie if you take my meaning."

"You mean ..."

He nodded. "Yeah. It's sick if you ask me, but it exists. And people will pay big bucks to see it."

"It's real?" Rick asked. "There are movies out there where some poor girl is murdered and people beat off to that?"

The man shrugged. "Like I said. All kinds of kinks for all kinds of folks."

"How do you know so much about it all if you don't touch that kind of stuff?" Rick asked.

"I know people who know people. The sex industry is well connected and believe me, what you see on Hollywood Boulevard is just the tip of the iceberg."

"Just a minute," Diane said, a sick feeling enveloping her insides and turning them to mush. "Ed Milton, the private detective, contacted you about these snuff movies?"

"Yeah. He wanted to view one. Part of some missing persons case he was working on. He knew Muscado made this stuff and he wanted to check one out. I heard that somebody was putting on a screening down in San Diego and I offered to put him in touch. But after that all I got from this Milton character was radio silence. I didn't know he was dead. I guess somebody got wise to him poking around."

"Who is this 'Muscado'?" asked Rick.

"How the hell should I know? Some filmmaker who makes this stuff. You think these guys use their real names?"

"Nobody knows who he is?"

"Somebody does, I guess. But it's all top secret. He makes the movies and sells them to another group who screen them for paying customers."

"Put us in contact with these people," said Rick.

"Why, so you can end up dead too? Look, these people aren't to be messed with. I heard Muscado's movies really go the extra mile. Real nutty stuff. Like *occult* stuff."

"Occult?" asked Diane.

"Yeah, robes and candles and pentagrams and all that jazz. I guess the freaks like that kind of drama."

"We want to see one of these films," Rick insisted.

"Look, I don't wanna stick my neck out further than it already is. They might have already tied that private detective to me. I don't wanna end up like him ..."

He was starting to panic and Rick seized him by his oversized lapels and dragged him halfway across the counter. "Listen, pal. My wife's sister is missing and if she's involved in this snuff shit then we want to know. We're not in it for a paycheck so don't think we're going to give up. And if you won't help us then perhaps the police will now that we've got some juicy information about what goes on behind closed doors in this part of town. You get me?"

"OK, Man, OK!" the man gibbered. "Lemme go!"

Rick released him and he took three steps backwards, rearranging his lapels and clearing his throat nervously. "All right, I can put you in touch with somebody. But for the love of Christ, don't let on that I knew anything about your missing sister. I don't wanna know about her and I never heard nothing about her. As far as I'm concerned, you're just a potential customer I sent their way."

"Like you did Ed Milton," Diane said.

"Yeah. Like that."

"How do we do this?"

"You do nothing for the time being," the man said. "I'll make the calls then I'll tell you where to go. You gotta understand that this is all very hush-hush. I don't know what kind of operation they run down there but the way I understand it, you won't see anybody's face. This shit is so deep it's unreal, you dig?"

"How will you let us know?" Rick asked. "We don't have a number you can call. We just got to L.A."

"Come back here tomorrow evening. I should have it all hooked up by then. And let's get serious, only you can go down there to see this thing. Leave the lady at home, huh?"

"We're in this together," Diane said. "It's *my* sister."

"Get real. If I send those boys a married couple they'll definitely know something's up. Bringing your old lady to a store like this is one thing but this is strictly a man's world, you know what I'm saying?"

"Sure," said Rick. He turned to Diane. "He has a point. I'll go and check this film out, whatever it is."

Diane bit her lip and said nothing until they had left the store. The sun had vanished now and the streets seemed busier with the burgeoning creatures of the night. "Rick, I feel sick!" she said.

He put his arm around her and pulled her close as they walked back to the Winnebago. "I know, Honey. I know."

"I can't believe Christine is mixed up in this snuff business. I just can't believe it."

"Me neither. But it could all be bullshit. Maybe these flicks aren't real. Maybe it's all make believe for some sickos who think it's real. Or maybe Christine isn't involved at all and Milton was on the wrong path. Or maybe he was working some other case. We just don't know."

"But we've got to find out," Diane said.

When they got back to the camper they headed out of town and found a campground off the Santa Ana Freeway. It had a pool and a run-down little rest area. Several campers were parked up but there didn't seem to be much life in them. Maybe folks had decided on an early night. That wasn't such a bad idea, Diane considered.

Rick had picked up a new bottle of bourbon from a liquor store and was in the business of cracking it open while Diane put the polaroid of Christine back in the box file along with the rest of the evidence. He was really hitting the bottle these days. And ever since the incident with those kids in the van, he had been on edge like never before. She guessed it had unnerved him more than he liked to admit.

She went into the dinette to wash up the things left over from breakfast. "Say, Rick?" she said. "Have you seen my marigolds?"

CHAPTER 5

Rick had another nightmare that night. He was back in the cave at nine years old, holding the gray man's hand. There were people all around him, hooded and robed, holding torches that illuminated the walls of the cave.

But it was no cave. The walls were regular and flat. They were blackened with age and encrusted with graffiti. Pentagrams and inverted crossed daubed in red paint ran down the brickwork like blood. The people were chanting and he could hear dogs barking and howling from some other part of the darkness.

He awoke with a start, aware that he had been uttering mumbled cries of protest. Diane was sitting up in her bed, looking at him, any trace of concern on her face hidden by darkness.

"Are you alright?" she asked.

"Yeah," he said, flopping his head back down on the pillow. "Nightmare, that's all. What time is it?"

Diane held her watch to the sliver of moonlight peeping in from behind the curtain and said; "A little after six."

They spoke no more, and Diane soon fell back to sleep. Rick lay awake, staring at the ceiling of the camper, going through his dream and trying to find the meaning in it. What he thought had been a cave in his previous dream was now revealed to be a manmade structure. *Like the pumphouse in Untermeyer Park*. It was the only thing he could think of that fit. He had been found outside that old ruin. What the hell had gone on inside it?

It was like things were being revealed to him in his dreams, one layer at a time, like peeling an onion. Was he remembering more of what he had repressed as a child? Or was all this talk about Christine joining some cult and getting mixed up in sick pornos messing with his head? Putting images there that never happened? Who knew how the hell the mind worked?

The sun rose and the heat within the camper grew stifling, even with the windows open. Rick got up, flung the door open and put on some coffee. When it was done, he sat outside and watched the day dawn over the hills. Another camper had arrived in the night and pulled up next to theirs. It was an old silver Airstream trailer pulled by tatty station wagon. Rick was surprised they had not been woken by its arrival.

Nobody else was up and about and the pool was still as glass. It was a peaceful scene marred by the drone of cars passing up and down the nearby freeway. The smell of the eucalyptus trees planted as windbreaks for the orange groves was mingled with the acrid stench of exhaust fumes. This contrast between the old world of ancient hills where the coyote had once howled and the ever-expanding modernity of freeways, motels campgrounds and theme parks made him feel depressed.

Pull yourself together, he scolded himself. *Now is not the time for self-pity or navel gazing*. Tonight, he would have to return to the sordid underbelly of Hollywood's sex industry and delve even further into the muck with God-only-knew-what waiting for him at the end of it. He had to keep it together, for Diane's sake.

But it was damn hard to stay on target, that was for sure. He was still so jittery after the previous night's events. The image of the three dead teenagers in the back of their van, his own axe embedded in the skull of one of them, slippery with blood, haunted his every waking hour.

He had disposed of the murder weapon the day before when they had been on their way to their appointment with Detective Garrett. They had pulled over at a gas station and, after they had tanked up, Diane had gone inside to buy some essentials. Rick had taken the opportunity to remove the axe from the storage locker and carry it over to a ditch that ran behind the gas station. He had hoped to find the ditch brimming with water but in high summer it was dry as a bone. There was a culvert and enough tangled weeds and dead grass to hide the package from view and he did a fair job of concealing it. Somebody would find it eventually, but they would be back in New York by then and it would take a first-grade detective to tie it to the murders.

It was a great relief to be free of the weapon. It had been driving him crazy knowing that it lay wrapped in a bloodied blanket in the storage locker and he was damn glad it was gone before they had parked up outside the Orange County Sheriff's Department. He didn't know if his nerves could take sitting down with a cop knowing that a murder weapon was in his possession. Somebody would have found that van by now and the cops would be looking for the murderer but there was nothing that tied him to it. He was in the clear, he knew that, but his nerves still hadn't got the message.

His armpit throbbed and he absentmindedly reached under it. There was a swelling there that was painful to the touch. Probably an infected gland or something. That might account for why he felt so damn hot and weak all the time. It was no wonder he was coming down with something with all that had happened and on top of that, these damn nightmares ruining his sleep.

The door to the neighboring camper opened and a woman in her early-thirties emerged wearing a wraparound dress with a vibrant print that was tight enough to show some rather nice curves. She had blonde hair tied in plaits and wore several bangles and necklaces. She looked like a relic from the hippie days of the previous decade and, judging by her age, Rick guessed that she was.

"Hi there!" she called upon spotting him. "Beautiful morning, huh?"

"Sure is," said Rick.

"You alone?"

"No, my wife is still asleep."

"Oh. I travel alone."

Rick said nothing.

"Where are you guys from?"

"New York."

"Far out. You on vacation?"

"Something like that. Yourself?"

"Oh yeah, I'm on the road. Have been for a while now. I'm bumming around Orange County for a while, visiting friends, seeing the sights, you know? L.A. is just a nightmare now."

"You got that right."

"Out here it's beautiful, if you get off the freeway that is. I was up in the Santa Ana mountains all last week sketching. I'm an artist. I have a studio back in Phoenix but sometimes I just need to get out and see nature. See the world!"

"What sort of art do you make?"

"A bit of everything. I don't constrain myself to any medium or style. Are you guys heading north?"

"San Diego actually. We decided to rest up here for a few days, take it easy."

"Sure. Me too. My name's Brenda, by the way."

"Rick."

"Pleased to meet you. Maybe we'll get to know each other if we're both going to be here for a few days. I was at a spot on my own last night and that's no joke. You heard about those murders?"

"Uh, yeah ..."

"A waitress with her heart cut out in Santa Ana?"

"Right. I did hear that."

"It makes me feel a whole lot safer being around people. Especially if there's a man next door. Anyway, look, I gotta take a shower. We'll talk more later, huh?"

"I'd like that."

Diane appeared at the doorway just in time for Brenda to catch her eye. The two women gave each other a brief smile of acknowledgement before Brenda headed off towards the concrete shower block down by the pool.

"Who was that?" Diane asked.

"Just our neighbor. Brenda."

"She was pretty."

"I didn't notice. She's an artist."

"You must have had quite the conversation."

"Oh, it was mostly on her side. I'm not quite feeling myself yet."

"Rough night?"

"Yeah. Too damn hot. And this day looks to get even hotter. Coffee's on the stove."

"Super."

After her first cup, Diane fixed them a breakfast of scrambled eggs and toast. When they were done eating, they decided to take a trip to the nearest town and stock up on some groceries. As they had nothing to do until their appointment with the owner of the sex shop later that evening, it was almost like they could pretend they were on vacation.

Once they had purchased their groceries, Rick decided that he was going to call his dad. While Diane was putting away their supplies, he went in search of a payphone. He knew why he had the sudden urge to speak to the old man. The nightmares he had been having were giving him a dark nostalgia for his youth and questions were beginning to surface like dead leaves at the bottom of a pond.

"Hey Dad, it's me," he said once the connection was established.

"Oh, hey Rick. How's it going out there?"

"Oh, not too bad. We made it to California. Not much of a vacation, but then I guess I shouldn't have expected one."

"Have you found out anything? Diane mentioned some cop she was going to meet ..."

"Yeah, we've been asking around but nobody seems to know anything. I don't have high hopes to tell you the truth. I think that private investigator found out all there was to be found."

"I guess so. It'll be hard on Diane. She won't want to give up."

"I know. Look, Dad, I have a question for you."

"Shoot, Son."

"You know when I went missing when I was a kid? Did they ever check out the old pump house in Untermeyer Park?"

"Sure they did. They checked out the whole area looking for whoever took you. Why do you ask?"

"Was there anything strange about that old building?"

"It was an old derelict even back then. Covered in graffiti and littered with trash. Cops said it was a hangout for local teenagers looking for somewhere to smoke dope and get frisky."

"What kind of graffiti?"

"Pentagrams and other witchy stuff. Just kids fooling around. Why the sudden interest?"

"Nothing. Just been thinking about it all."

"Well, don't dwell on it. We got you back, that's the important thing. Not a day went by that your mother didn't give thanks to the Lord for your safe return."

"Yeah. Thanks, Dad."

"Anytime son. Good luck with your search. If you came back to us, then Diane's sister might. You just have to have faith, that's what your mother would have said."

After he had hung up, Rick stood in the phone booth a while, staring at the receiver. He hadn't imagined the satanic graffiti in the pump house. It had really been there. And he must have seen it at age nine and kept it with him all these years only to remember it in a dream now. Did that mean that the hooded figures and the barking dogs had also been there? And what else had he repressed? What else lay lurking in the back of his subconscious, waiting to burst forth in feverish nightmares?

They spent the rest of the day lounging around back at the camping ground. Brenda came over and introduced herself to Diane. There was a coolness between the two women and Rick could tell that Diane didn't like Brenda all that much.

With the onset of evening, they headed back into Los Angeles. After a brief discussion in a Walgreen's parking lot, it was decided that Rick would go in alone. He left Diane smoking a cigarette in the passenger seat, gazing at the prostitutes walking up and down the boulevard, and headed over to the 'love emporium'.

The manager was deep in conversation with a customer regarding an order of some sort of 'plug' that turned Rick's ears crimson to hear about. He tried to make himself look busy by browsing the magazine racks. Nothing he saw there helped ease his acute sense of discomfort. He felt the swelling under his armpit. It sure was sore the way his shirt rubbed against it. And by God, was it hot in here?

The customer eventually left, and Rick made his way over to the counter.

"Butt plugs," the manager said, jabbing his pen at the notepad he had been scribbling on. "Got a big order coming in on Thursday. Can I interest you? Special discount?"

"Cut the crap," Rick said. "Have you got anything for me?"

"Yeah. I called my man. As luck would have it, they're having a screening the day after tomorrow. Midnight, Wednesday. San Diego. A hundred bucks a ticket."

"A hundred? To see a movie? You gotta be kidding!"

"I tried to tell you, man, this stuff is hardcore, outta this world, rarer than rare shit. And thank God for that if you ask me. The risks these characters run in showing this stuff are sky high. You think they're gonna charge the same as the porno theatre next door? The people who want this stuff *really* want it, you dig? And they're willing to pay. Question is, are you?"

Rick thought about it. It was bad enough to have to go and sit through this thing – whatever it was – but to lay down a hundred big ones for the privilege? But then, he knew Diane would pay any price to find out what happened to Christine. This was their only lead and he couldn't screw this up for her now.

"All right," he said. "I pay them, right? I'm not expected to fork over the dough to you, am I?"

"No, you pay them on the night in question," the manager said.

"But you'll get your kickback no doubt," said Rick.

"Do I ask you about your business?"

"Take it easy. You got an address for me?"

"Sure, here you go." He jotted down a street address in San Diego, tore it off his pad and slid it over to Rick.

"Any password I should know?"

"What do you think this is? *The Man from Uncle*? You just show up and do what you're told. And remember our agreement; I know nothing about this girl you're looking for. You're just some guy who wants to see a snuff film, got it?"

"Sure."

"Have a blast."

Rick left the store, folded up the piece of paper with the address on it, and slipped it into his shirt pocket.

With two days to kill before they had to head down to San Diego, Rick and Diane suddenly found themselves with free time on their hands that they were utterly unprepared for. They spent the next day milling around and by the second day, the campground had livened up somewhat as the vacation season hit its stride. The pool roared with the sound of kids playing and splashing. Rick and Diane were just starting to discuss dinner plans when Brenda came strolling up from the pool, towel over her shoulder. Rick was glad he was wearing sunglasses for he couldn't stop his eyes from roving over her lovely body which her bikini left little to imagine.

"You guys not going in the pool?" Brenda asked.

"Little too crowded for me," said Diane. "And Rick hates swimming."

"Really? Why?"

"I don't *hate* swimming," Rick protested, not liking the way his wife made him out to be some sort of spoilsport. "We were just discussing heading out for dinner. We're leaving tomorrow, you see."

"Oh, you're leaving so soon?"

"Yeah, we have an appointment in San Diego," said Rick, not wanting to go into all the details with Brenda but not really knowing what else to tell her. Who the hell takes their vacation in San Diego, anyway?

"An appointment, huh? So this isn't just a vacation for you?"

"Not exactly," said Diane. "The truth is, we're looking for my sister." The polaroid appeared as if by magic. "She went off to California with some boyfriend and now we've lost track of her. We think she might be in danger."

"Oh boy, a mystery, huh?" said Brenda, examining the polaroid. "Well, I haven't seen her in my travels."

"We didn't mean to ask you if you had," said Rick, keen to assure Brenda that they weren't grilling her. "But we've gotten so used to flashing her picture to folks that it comes as second nature."

"Sure, of course. And you never know, you might get lucky. Somebody will have seen her. She's a cute kid. How old?"

"Eighteen and convinced that she's old enough to explore the world," said Diane.

"I was eighteen when I ran off," said Brenda. "And I turned out OK. I'm sure your sister is fine. Why are you headed to San Diego? Has somebody seen her there?"

"Well, not exactly," said Rick, now feeling that they were definitely in a no-go area of conversation. "But somebody who may have seen her lives there. We just want to ask them a few questions."

"Who saw her?"

Rick and Diane were silent, a little put out by the sudden directness of the question.

"I'm sorry, I'm prying," said Brenda. "I only meant to help. The more people who know ... you know? Look, if tonight is to be your last night then I insist on having you both round for dinner."

"Oh, you don't have to do that ..." Diane began."

"I said I insist. Besides, traveling alone is a blast but the evenings do get lonely. I'd love some dinner companions for once."

"Well, then sure," said Rick, suddenly aware of Diane glaring at him. "What time do you want us?"

"Oh, just pop over whenever you're ready. It won't be anything fancy, I'm afraid. I don't have much of a kitchenette and only a few bits and pieces to throw together."

"We'll be there."

"Terrific!" She headed into her trailer and Rick averted his eyes from her very watchable backside.

"Why did you agree to that?" Diane hissed at him once Brenda had closed the door to her trailer. "We don't want to have dinner with her!"

"Why the hell not? She's seems perfectly nice."

"Nice? Oh, I'm sure she's nice. But she's hardly our sort, is she?"

"Our *sort*? When did you get so snobby?"

Diane huffed at this but said nothing.

They knocked on the door of Brenda's camper at around seven. She opened it with an open bottle of wine in one hand and two glasses in the other. She was wearing a turquoise dress with coral and shell jewelry and Rick was put in mind of a golden-haired mermaid emerging from her underwater cave.

"Come in!" she said, brandishing the bottle. "Do you like red? I've not brought much of a wine cellar with me, I'm afraid."

"Red's fine," said Rick holding up their own offering. "We brought a bottle too so we shouldn't run out."

"Terrific!"

The interior of Brenda's caravan was like some bohemian pad in Greenwich Village. A tie-die sheet screened the sleeping compartment and the bland vinyl seating area had been spruced up with multi-hued throws and Indian cushions. Jars of shells and brightly colored pebbles were arranged by the windows.

She'd certainly made an effort with the dinner. They had melon balls and Parma ham for a starter and then a chicken fricassee with dumplings for the main followed by pudding and canned pineapple for desert. Brenda's hippie aesthetic had worried Rick that she might be a vegetarian but the meal was excellent and even Diane seemed pleasantly surprised.

They talked about New York and California and Brenda regaled them with tales of her travels and the weird people and things she had seen. She told them about her art studio back in Arizona and the kind of stuff she was sketching out here in California.

"You're originally from Arizona?" Rick asked her.

"No, I'm from Cali. I just moved out there after the whole scene burned out ten years ago. I was a real hippie chick, if you can believe it. Lived in Haight-Ashbury for a while before heading down to L.A. Crazy times but the scene turned sour. Biker gangs started running the show, pimping the girls and pushing bad drugs. Too many crazies running around."

"Like the Manson Family," Rick prompted.

"Yeah, that was the real nail in the coffin lid," said Brenda. "And I was lucky not to get caught up in that mess. I worked on a commune with one of the Manson girls back in '67. A couple of years later I see her on the news as one of the girls who murdered that poor Sharon Tate woman. But for the grace of God, know what I mean?"

"Yeah, you dodged a bullet there," said Rick.

"That's when I decided to quit California. I met a guy from Arizona and we lived together for a while but it didn't last. I had already set up my studio by then so I just stayed put."

"But you were drawn back to California," said Diane.

"Yeah, only on vacation. I'd never live here again but there's just too much artistic inspiration here. It's the ancient places that drew me to the Santa Ana mountains. As an artist, those hills and their ruins are springs of inspiration. They have such a power in them, don't you think?"

"Well, I'm afraid our own experience in the Santa Ana mountains was a little less majestic," said Diane. "We were nearly run off the road by some crazy kids in their van a couple of days ago."

"You're kidding!" said Brenda, her innocent eyes wide. "Did you call the cops?"

"No, we were going to but Rick put on his tough guy act and gave them hell. Didn't have any trouble from them after that."

"Can I see some of your sketches?" Rick asked, keen to change the topic.

"Oh, sure," Brenda replied, getting up to fetch a large sketchpad from her sleeping compartment. "They're pretty rough but I think I captured the primal essence of the places."

She scooted in next to Rick until she was practically sitting in his lap. Rick glanced uneasily at Diane who watched them with an icy stare. Brenda began to leaf through the sketch pad, showing him penciled depictions of mountainsides, waterfalls and pine forests. Abandoned ranches and adobe ruins were hauntingly brought to life in black and white, their deep shadows concealing any number of ancient secrets.

"You're good," he told her.

"Thank you."

He was aware of her scent; some strange perfume in her hair, and the warmth of her thigh against his. He tried not to look too comfortable, conscious of Diane sitting not three feet from them.

Brenda seemed to suddenly remember Diane's presence too and quickly focused on her. "Tell me more about your missing sister," she said, folding away her sketch pad. "Like I said, the more people who know about her, the more likely it is she'll turn up. I'll be travelling around quite a bit so you never know. I might hear something."

"Well, the last we heard, she was headed up to O'Neill Park," said Diane. "Apparently she knew some movie business folk who had a ranch up there."

"That's where I've just been! O'Neill Park is a known spot for wild teenagers to hang out. I should know, I used to be one of them! But those days are behind me. Now I just go up there for the scenery."

"Well, we plan to take a look around there when we get back from San Diego," said Diane.

"What are you looking for down there anyway?" Brenda asked.

"Chasing down a lead. The private detective we hired uncovered something to do with the porn racket."

Brenda frowned. "Sounds like a bit of a long shot. If your sister was anything like me then she would have steered clear of all that. Believe me, there's enough in O'Neill Park to satisfy young and adventurous minds. You'd be best off looking for leads there."

"Thanks anyway," said Diane a little coldly. "But we need to chase down *every* lead. We're not leaving any stone unturned."

"Oh, I understand," said Brenda. "Look, I hope you find your sister, really, but try not to worry too much. A lot of us flower children escaped the sixties unscathed. She's probably having the time of her life and just needs the space to get it all out of her system. She'll rear her head when she's good and ready. Most of us do."

"She was flirting with you!" said Diane in an accusatory voice once they were back in their own camper.

"What?" Rick exclaimed as he loosened his tie and tossed it into the sleeping compartment.

"Don't act like you didn't notice!"

"Oh, come on! You're jealous of some hippie chick?"

"I would hardly call her a 'chick'. She's at least a couple of years older than us."

"Really? I'd say she was thirty-ish."

"That's not the point. The point is that she was flirting with you and you lapped it up!"

"I did not!"

"And she even tried to tell us not to go to San Diego. As if Christine is anything like her! I'm just glad we'll be gone tomorrow. I don't like that woman one bit."

Figures, thought Rick as they undressed and climbed into their separate beds. *Somebody notices that I'm a red-blooded male for once and you don't like it.*

He lay down, his head buzzing with the wine they had drunk. It was so damned hot! The throbbing in his armpit was worse. He felt the lump there and noticed that it had gotten bigger. Jesus, was he going to have to visit a doctor now? That's all they needed.

Chapter 6

The address the manager of the Love Boutique had given Rick was for a warehouse in the Midway area; a district of grimy motels, adult bookstores, and auto repair shops that shrank from the lights of the nearby San Diego Sports Arena. It was some old warehouse with a chain-link fence surrounding the lot and a yellow barrier blocking the entrance. There wasn't a sign of life about the place and, for a moment, Rick was worried that he had been given the wrong address or that the showing of the movie had moved location.

"This is it, Bud," said the taxi driver.

"Just wait a minute," Rick said.

"It's your money, Bud."

A black Cadillac was heading down the street towards them. Rick and the taxi driver were briefly bathed in light as it turned down a dim alley between two colossal buildings. The red of its rear lights winked out and Rick realized that the driver must have parked.

Somebody emerged from the alley, a slim fellow with a snap brim hat pulled low at the front, shielding his face from the taxi's headlights. He hurried across the road towards the barrier and a figure partially emerged from the darkness of the lot to greet him. Some words were exchanged, and the man was admitted.

Guess this is the place after all.

Rick paid the taxi driver and got out. He watched the lights of the taxi disappear down the street with a sinking feeling. He was on his own now in this godforsaken part of a strange city. He walked across the broken asphalt towards the barrier. He could just make out the glowing end of a cigarette burning in the darkness; the only indicator that somebody was there.

"What's your business here?" the man at the barrier said.

"I ... uh. I'm here to see the movie?" Rick said, not knowing if this was at all the correct thing to say."

"Do you work for the San Diego Police Department?" The man asked.

"No, of course not," Rick replied.

"Do you have any kind of affiliation to any other law enforcement agencies?"

"No."

"Proceed. The yellow door next to the loading dock."

Feeling like he had passed some sort of test, Rick walked around the barrier and crossed the parking lot towards the rear of the building. *What if I was a cop?* He wondered. *Would I have to declare it? Even if I was working undercover?* He thought he had read somewhere that cops couldn't lie to people about being cops. Something called 'entrapment'. These characters were obviously trying to cover their asses by flat-out asking everybody who showed up.

The yellow door was closed and he wondered if he should knock. The guy at the barrier hadn't said anything about knocking. He decided to show some backbone and walk right in. The door was stiff and opened onto a dimly lit corridor. Rick followed it to its end and noticed the busted punch clock on the wall and its rack of yellowing timecards. This warehouse had been abandoned long ago. It was clear to him now how this group ran its operation. They'd screen their illegal movies in obscure locations like this one, probably for one night only and then move on. *Untraceable.*

As he rounded the corner he came to a stairwell. A pair of fire doors were padlocked so he ventured upstairs. He found himself in what had been the warehouse's cafeteria. A few tables and chairs were stacked up against one wall and the checkered linoleum was marked where vending machines had once stood. Several figures occupied the room – Rick couldn't be sure how many – sitting on plastic chairs in the gloom at its far end.

The only light in the room was behind the counter where lunch had once been served to the warehouse's workers. Two men in Halloween masks were sitting there, a cash box brimming with green notes open in front of them. One was Dracula and the other Batman. The situation seemed so absurd that Rick could have laughed if he momentarily forgot the danger and illegality of it all.

"A hundred bucks," said Batman. "Then take a seat. The movie is about to begin. Don't look at anybody, don't talk to anybody."

"Right," said Rick, his hand going into his jacket pocket and drawing out the wad of bills. Jesus, was he really doing this? He handed the cash over and Dracula quickly counted it. He noticed a sawed-off shotgun resting on the countertop next to the open money box. These guys weren't kidding around.

At a nod from the plastic-faced count, Rick sauntered across the room to where an empty seat awaited him. The other customers seemed preoccupied with their feet or their fingernails, all of them keen to show their disinterest in who he was or what he looked like. He tried to return the favor.

He seemed to have been the last to arrive for, just as he sat down, a man in the darkness somewhere behind him turned on a projector. As it whirred into life, illuminating the dust particles in the air, a square of light was thrown onto the bare wall of the cafeteria, grainy and flickering.

There was a nervous clearing of throats as the anticipation in the room built and Rick began to regret getting into all of this. What the hell was he about to see? What if it was Christine up there on the screen? What if he was about to watch her get killed? But he had to be strong. If their worst fears were confirmed tonight, then he had to sit it out and try and remember everything in the film; everything and anything that might be a clue that they could pass on to the police.

The film started with a flicker of color and they were afforded a view of somewhere outdoors beneath a brilliant sunset. Hills were visible in the distance and Rick had no doubt that this had been shot somewhere in California.

The camera panned and focused on a naked woman on all fours. She was wearing a hood that looked like it was made of black silk. Her back was arched and her buttocks thrust outwards. There was no sound, only the clicking of the projector and the polite cough of somebody behind Rick trying to conceal their arousal.

Even with a hood on, Rick could see that this girl was not Christine. Some hair was visible beneath the edge of the hood and it was dark brown. Christine was blonde. The relief he felt at this did not linger. He knew that this was somebody's daughter, somebody's sister. That he did not know her had little bearing on his fear of what was about to happen to her.

More robed figures appeared, and they led an unhooded female between them who staggered, as if drunk. She had her back to the camera and had shoulder-length blonde hair. Rick froze. Was this Christine?

The robed figures turned the girl around and Rick almost let out a gasp of relief when he saw that this girl wasn't Christine either. He was so damn jumpy with all this bait-and-switch that he didn't know how much more of this he could take.

The blonde girl was laid down on the back of the hooded girl whose kneeling form made her into a kind of table. Ropes were brought forth to bind the two girls together, hands to hands and feet to feet, so that the blonde girl's back was arched and her belly thrust upwards. One of the robed figures stood behind her while a candle, a bell and a goblet was placed on her quivering belly. Rick had heard of this sort of thing. It was called a black mass; a perverted parody of the Catholic ritual.

Then the robed congregation began a monophonic Gregorian chant and Rick was suddenly aware that the film had a soundtrack. He had been expecting some grainy 8mm film but this was high-budget stuff.

As the chanting continued, Rick was suddenly over-come by a sickening sense of familiarity. He had heard those very same chants before, in his deepest nightmares. Perhaps he had heard them at the tender age of nine, in the pumphouse in Untermeyer Park. Could this be the same group of characters? Had some sort of cult that had operated in Yonkers in the 1950s now moved to California? Or was it a different group involved in the same scene? How widespread was this thing?

He quickly abandoned his ruminations when the ritual being acted out on celluloid began to heat up. The hooded figures knelt at the side of the perverted altar, their hands on the naked body of the bound woman, pawing at her, squeezing her breasts and rubbing the soft fuzz of her sex.

Somebody behind Rick seemed to be struggling with something and he realized that the constricted grunts were the primal sounds of masturbation. *Jesus*, he thought. *They actually whack off to this stuff.*

Then, the apparent priest of the gathering drew a knife from the folds of his robes. It was a short, ugly thing that looked like it belonged in a museum of prehistoric cultures. Its blade was black and jagged as if it had been hacked into sharpness rather than ground by a whet-stone. With more Latin declarations, he held the knife aloft like some sort of talisman.

The chanting stopped. A pregnant silence reigned both in the film and in the audience. The priest lowered the knife and pressed it to the taught neck of the bound girl. The camera zoomed in. The audience held its breath. Rick squirmed in his seat, wishing he could leave, not wanting to see any more.

The priest dragged the jagged blade across the neck of the girl, tearing open her jugular. Blood spurted from the wound and the golden goblet was held out to catch most of it. The girl writhed in fear and pain, her hands and legs jerking impotently at their bindings. The hooded woman beneath her held firm, her own head and shoulders red with the blood of the sacrifice.

The gush of expended excitement was audible all around Rick as his fellow viewers gasped in appreciation. He felt glued to his chair, stuck in some nightmare he did not know how to awake from. There was no doubt that the thing on screen was real. He had seen his share of drive-in movies to see through their corny special effects. No, this was the real deal. They were watching the real murder of a real girl.

The cultists began to disrobe, keeping their hoods on. They were men and women, mostly young but there were a few old ones evidenced by sagging muscles and slack skin. The golden goblet was passed around and they began smearing themselves and each other in the blood of the girl. She was dead now, Rick was pretty sure. She no longer moved. Her head hung back, the weight of it pulling open the gash in her neck like a hideous second mouth.

The camera pulled back to reveal more of the blood orgy. The hooded creatures were red from neck to toe as they writhed like a pit of serpents. The sun was setting over the ghastly scene and, silhouetted against the darkening sky, was a tower of some kind. From what Rick could see, it had many sides that made it either a hexagon or an octagon. It was in poor shape and in keeping with the ruined nature of what little else Rick had seen of the ghastly film's shooting location. These crazies had undoubtedly chosen the location for its gothic resemblance to a horror movie but there was something familiar about it. He felt as if he had seen that tower somewhere before.

The picture suddenly vanished as the reel ran out and they were left looking at a flickering square of light on the far wall.

It was like waking from a nightmare. Rick's surroundings slowly slid back into his consciousness. The rest of the audience was stirring. Dark figures rose around him and began making their way towards the stairwell. Nobody turned the lights on. Batman and Dracula had made themselves scarce and the cash box and the shotgun were gone from the counter. Even the cameraman had vanished into the recesses of the building.

Rick waited until he was alone and then didn't hang about any longer than necessary. He rose on shaking legs and commanded them to carry him in the wake of the last figure who had left. He could hear footsteps echoing in the stairwell and he had never wanted to be out of a place so badly in his life.

He hurried down the stairs and made his way along the corridor in time to catch the heavy door before it swung closed. He stepped out into the night air and breathed deeply, trying to calm his jumping nerves and ward off the swelling nausea in his belly. Everybody had vanished back into the shadows of the city. Even the cigarette-smoking guard at the barrier was gone.

Rick made his way out of the lot and into the unhealthy yellow of the streetlights. He needed to call a cab somehow and get back to Diane, back to sanity if any such thing existed after what he had seen.

But it hadn't been Christine.

The relief at not having their worst fears confirmed seemed intent on eluding him. It was true; Christine had made no appearance in the film and therefore, might still be alive. Despite the gut-wrenching experience he had just been through, the night had to be considered a success, surely?

Then why the hell had Milton been chasing this film? If Christine was somehow connected to this world, then she might still be in danger. He had seen a different girl murdered but that didn't prove that Christine hadn't been murdered in some other film. How many of these things were floating about?

He tried to stay positive. Christine hadn't been in the snuff movie. He knew that would keep Diane's hopes alive, at least for the time being. But wherever Christine was, time might be running out for her. As much as his mind recoiled at the thought, they had to get deeper into this world, dig further into the muck.

That tower ...

Yes. The tower. He had seen something that might give them some clue as to where these sickos made their murder movies. A strange tower like that had to stick out in the California hills. He was sure he had seen it somewhere recently. Had they driven past it in the camper? If only he could remember ...

He made it to a nearby motel and called a cab which took him back to Diane. It was past two and he was dog tired. As he sat in the camper's dinette and poured out a much-needed drink for himself, Diane sat opposite him, her eyes eagerly awaiting his report on the night's proceedings.

"It wasn't her, Diane," he said. "It wasn't Christine."

"You're sure?" Diane asked, clearly reluctant to celebrate prematurely.

"It was some other poor girl. Blonde, like Christine, but not her. I got a good look at her face before they ..."

"You mean they really ...?"

"Oh yeah. The film really delivered in that regard. It was some sort of satanic shit with a high priest and everything. It was a blood sacrifice."

"Don't!" said Diane, holding up a hand. "It wasn't Christine, that's all I need to know. But I think I'll join you for a drink. My nerves need it after waiting up for you all night."

"There's something else," Rick said after polishing off his drink and holding it out for Diane to refill. "I saw something in the background. A tower built on a promontory or something. It was a ruin."

"Well, we have no idea where the film was shot so that's like looking for a needle in a haystack."

"It was California."

"How can you be sure?"

"I've seen enough of its desert hills in the past week to recognize the Golden State. And besides, there was something familiar about it. Like I'd seen it before somewhere. There can't be that many ruins about. We just need to ... wait! Hold on just a minute!"

"What is it?" Diane asked.

"I know where I've seen that tower!"

"Where?"

"Brenda's sketchbook!"

Diane narrowed her eyes at the mention of Brenda's name.

"That crazy hippie said she'd been travelling all through Orange County sketching old ruins. I saw that tower in her sketchbook!"

"Are you sure?"

"Sure I'm sure. She's a good artist and she penciled that damned thing just as I saw it in the movie. Probably from the same angle too. She must have stood right there where they sacrificed the girl. Now where was it she said she had been before she met us?"

"O'Neill Park."

"Jesus, isn't that where Christine went?"

"Yes."

"So there might be a connection after all. Maybe Milton *was* on the right track."

Diane slammed her fist on the tabletop in frustration. Rick felt it too. Just when they thought they could forget the idea that Christine was somehow connected to these snuff movies, something else drew a red line between them.

"Well, you know what we have to do now, don't you?" Diane said.

"What?"

"We have to get back to that Brenda woman and find out where in O'Neill Park this tower is."

CHAPTER 7

"The murder weapon was most likely an axe," Detective Garrett said to Sheriff Baldwin. "The coroner figures it's a long-handled wood splitter."

"Mmm-hmm," Sheriff Baldwin said with a grim face as he sifted through the autopsy photos that had been delivered to his desk in a manilla envelope. His cigarette, forgotten between his fingers, was building up a good head of ash.

The pictures were as horrific as anything a cop was likely to see in a whole career, but they paled in comparison to the experience of seeing the crime scene in the flesh, to use a savory choice of words. Garrett would carry the memories of what he had seen in the back of that van until his dying day.

"And no such axe was found at the crime scene, am I right?" Sheriff Baldwin said, laying the last photograph face down on his desk.

"No, the weapon has not yet been recovered."

"Killer must have taken it with him. Any word on the victims' identities?"

"Yes, Detective Anderson has traced the van to an Andrew Marston in Santa Ana. His twenty-year-old kid, Craig Marston took off with it a couple of weeks ago. He hasn't reported it stolen because this has happened before. Kid seems like a bad seed. Pretty heavy into barbiturates and spends most of his time drifting about, sleeping on friends' couches. Anderson spoke to some of his friends who say that they saw him riding around with a couple of other kids; Stephen Martinson and Charlotte Bayer, both seventeen. Anderson is looking into it but they seem like a pretty good fit for the victims".

"Sounds like it. But kids out for kicks aren't usually targets for robbery."

"No, I think we can rule robbery out. There was no cash found in the van but they probably didn't have any to begin with. A bag of reds and some marijuana was found in the glove compartment so I'd say the killer wasn't even looking for anything. Besides, this level of brutality suggests a bloodlust being satisfied. The coroner said that he hasn't seen this kind of a rage in a murder in all his twenty years."

"I can double that," said Sheriff Baldwin. "Any connection to the Hillary and Munroe murders?"

"I don't figure it. These kids were hacked to pieces. Hillary and Monroe were beaten and strangled."

"Maybe he's stepped up his game?"

"I don't think so. Hillary and Munroe had their hearts removed. There was something ritualistic about their murders. This seems so ... savage. *Primal.*"

"Just my luck. Two goddamned maniacs on the loose in one summer. As if we're not stretched too thin already."

Unless one killer has taken care of another, Garrett thought. He didn't voice his opinion to the sheriff. It was a pretty outlandish theory and he knew Sheriff Baldwin was a man for facts and didn't take kindly to wild theorizing. But a large buck knife had also been found in the glove compartment of the Marston van. It had been cleaned but not well enough to completely remove a dark brownish residue where the blade met the handle. Garrett had sent it to forensics but he was pretty sure it was dried blood.

Then there was the footprint found near the body of the waitress, Hillary. The print indicated a Vans Deck shoe just like the pair of ragged blue shoes the late Craig Marston wore. Could these three kids have been the killers of Munroe and Hillary? Had it been these three teenage drifters who had murdered two women and then brutally mutilated their corpses in some dark satanic rite?

Who then, had ended their reign of terror? Such a person might be considered a hero if their own crime had not been so goddamned unhinged.

"Well whatever is going on, we need to get to the bottom of it," said Sheriff Baldwin. "The D.A. is on my ass and the papers are hauling us over the coals. Two killers on the loose! Goddamn it!"

That evening, Garrett met Detective Anderson at *Riley's*, an Irish bar in Tustin and a regular cop hangout. Garrett could already see two of his colleagues making good headway at the bar as he sidled into the booth Anderson had commandeered.

"Sheriff get the lowdown?" Anderson asked.

Garrett took a sip from his frosty mug of beer and nodded as he swallowed it.

"You tell him about the print?"

"No. I want us to be sure before we drop that bombshell. I'm still in the doghouse with him after that suicide at the Perks Motel."

"You still figure that P.I. was murdered?"

"I don't know. But with these new murders we're unlikely to find out. The boss wants this guy found ASAP. The only ray of light might be that these kids might've been the ones who killed Hillary and Monroe."

"I think they were. I showed the print to the boys in Irvine. They agree it's a match for Marston's shoe. The lab also got back to us about the knife. It's blood."

"Then it was Marston and his buddies who are our satanic killers," said Garrett, taking a celebratory gulp of beer.

"Pretty conclusive. I think you can take that to the boss and get out of the doghouse. With that news making the rounds, he'll be peachy. So will the D.A."

"Yeah, one set of murders solved, one to go. All we have to do now is find this second killer, whoever the hell he is. I can't figure the motive."

"Some sort of vigilante?"

"Who knows a hell of a lot more about these three kids than we do."

Garrett came in late the next morning. He'd barely slept. He poured himself some stale coffee and gulped half of it down.

"I was about to put on some fresh," said Detective Halloran, approaching him.

"It can't wait," Garrett said, grimacing.

"Rough night?"

"I was up 'til two talking to my sister-in-law."

"How is she?"

"She's fine. Her son, my dear nephew, is not."

"He in trouble again?"

"Smoking dope in school. They want to expel him."

"Can't they give the kid a break? He's so recently lost his father ..."

"Give him a break, give him a break. When do the rest of us get a break? Do you know his mother wants him to come and live with me?"

"You?" Halloran stifled a grin.

"Yeah, laugh it up, Jack. I might as well laugh too. I'm divorced with two grown up kids who know me about as well as they know Santa Claus. And yet somehow she thinks I'll be a good influence on the kid." He noticed the envelope in Halloran's hands. "You got something for me?"

"Yeah, this is the list of list of license plates we took from the owners of the San Juan Campground across from where the three bodies were found."

"Anything unusual?"

"Not that I can see. Just regular campers and a station wagon."

"I'll take a look."

Halloran gave him the envelope.

"Where's Anderson?"

"Taking a statement from a witness. Some lady at the roadhouse near Ortega Falls saw the blue van the day of the murders."

"Sounds promising." He gulped down the rest of the awful coffee and tossed the Styrofoam cup in the trash before heading into his office.

He sat down with a sigh and began reading through the list of license plates Halloran had drummed up for him. It was hard to focus. His mind kept wandering to his conversation with his dead brother's widow. He had done his best to help her after his brother's suicide two years ago and he knew it wasn't easy for a single mother and a teenage boy. But how did she expect the kid to do any better if she sent him to live with him? He worked all the hours God sent and wouldn't be able to keep an eye on the boy. Left to his own devices, dope smoking would be the least of their worries.

Jesus. What was it with kids these days? He tried to avoid drawing parallels between his nephew and the three dead teenagers but it was impossible. They were the same ages and by the sound of it, were into the same things, bar satanic murder (hopefully). His nephew was a good kid but if he kept up with the dope and the bad attitude, where was no telling where he would end up. The image of the mangled corpses in the back of the van flashed through his mind and he closed his eyes and tried to force it away.

Not for the first time in the past two years, he cursed his brother for blowing his brains out. *Goddamn you, Mike. You think the rest of us don't have it hard? Why did you get to take the easy way out and leave the rest of us to take care of things? Now your damned kid is going off the rails and I don't know what to do to stop him.*

The phone on his desk rang. It was Detective Anderson.

"We got a call from a woman who saw the Marston van," Anderson said.

"Yeah, Halloran told me," Garrett replied. "What's the story?"

"Apparently those three kids pulled in there and got into a scuffle with somebody. The guy was pretty mad and made some threats. Pushed them around and damn near slugged the Marston kid. He and his buddies didn't stick around and hightailed it out of there. This was the evening they got murdered."

"You're kidding."

"Nope. This guy, whoever he was, seems like a good fit. From what the witness understood, there was some sort of bother on the highway and he flipped his lid. Possible motive, don't you think?"

"Sure. Any lead on the guy?"

"He was there with his wife and they took off in a Winnebago. I've been up at the roadhouse canvassing. Nix on the make and model and nobody got the license, but someone thinks it was a New York plate."

"Wait a minute," said Garrett, cradling the receiver between his chin and collarbone as he shuffled through the files on his desk.

"Here!" he exclaimed. "A Winnebago with New York plates camped at the San Juan Campground on the night of the murders. Registered to a Richard Margold."

Margold? He thought. The name was familiar. Wasn't that the name of that couple who had come over from New York to look for the wife's little sister? Yeah, Diane Margold, that was it. He had her name written down somewhere.

"Get back to me if you find anything else out," he said to Anderson.

He hung up and sat back in his chair, gazing at the list of license plates. *Margold.* The couple who had hired the deceased private detective. The same couple who had a grievance against the Marston kid and his friends. The Marston kid and his friends who had murdered Hillary and Munroe and mutilated their bodies in satanic rituals. The Marston kid and his friends who had been brutally murdered in return by some maniac with an axe within spitting distance of where the Margolds had camped that night.

The trail went round in a circle and everything seemed connected but exactly how was a mystery to Garrett. All he knew was that there was something damned odd about the Margolds. Were they really looking for the wife's little sister? Or were they here in Orange County for some other, darker purpose? There was something ugly here, he was sure of it and he had to find out what it was.

CHAPTER 8

Brenda had moved on by the time they returned to the campground off the Santa Ana Freeway. Another family with two kids had taken her spot and the campground was a lot noisier than it had been a day ago. Rick and Diane spent a reluctant night there and at first light they headed east towards the rising sun and the sprawling hills of O'Neill Park.

They passed through the town of El Toro and picked up some groceries. Diane asked the storekeeper if the town had a public library and was directed to a small red brick building in what passed for the town center. They entered and found an elderly librarian stamping books behind his desk.

"Help you folks?" he asked, peering above his half-moon spectacles.

"Uh, yeah," said Diane. "We're researching local history and have heard about some old ruin in O'Neill Park."

"Plenty of old places to poke around in up there," said the librarian. "Indian, mostly. That what you're after?"

"No, I don't think so. This would be more of a mansion or a castle or something."

"Castle?" the librarian said with a glimmer of amusement. "Not much in the way of castles in O'Neill Park. Or Southern California for that matter. Where are you folks from?"

"New York, actually. We're here on vacation and I'm interested in architecture. Somebody described a place out here with a tower with several sides to it. They described it as a ruin but couldn't be sure. The tower juts out over a precipice."

The librarian sat back and raised his glasses to rest on his forehead. "Well now, that sounds like the old McCreedy place. But that's not in O'Neill Park, it's up Trabuco Canyon."

"And it has a multi-sided tower?"

"Sure does. It's a ruin too. Ever since it burned down in the forties."

"Well, that sounds hopeful," said Diane. "Could you possibly point us in the right direction?"

"I could point it out on a map for you, though I don't know what 'architecture' you hope to find there. The place is just some stones on a hillside these days."

Rick fetched the folding map from the camper and the librarian helpfully showed them where the old McCreedy place was. It was at the head of a trail that wound its way into the mountains north of Trabuco Canyon and looked to be in the middle of nowhere.

"Old Alister McCreedy was a strange sort," said the librarian. "Came to California in the 1920s and built that place jutting out of the hills like it was a mountain retreat. The fire was in '42 as I recall. He and his family burned alive. Ugly business."

They thanked the librarian and went back out to the camper.

"Sounds like the right place," said Diane as they got back in and started it up.

"If this is even what we should be looking for," said Rick.

O'Neill Park covered some four-thousand acres of the Santa Ana foothills and was a popular vacation spot with hikers, cyclists and horseback riders. As they drove along Trabuco Creek Road they passed several campers and station wagons loaded down with equipment as well as plenty of people on foot, bowed under the weight of backpacks and sleeping bags. Diane gazed at the golden hillsides and wooded valleys on their left, dappled by the sunlight shining through the leaves of the live oaks, and the park seemed nothing but serene. It was hard to imagine any kind of sordid darkness blighting its golden hillsides and wooded valleys but Diane knew it was there. Wherever the light was strongest, the shadows were deepest and she knew that something sinister lurked in those hills.

They wound their way up through Trabuco Canyon and into the trails of the foothills. Civilization seemed to fall away behind them as they reached the bleak heights of scrubland and twisted oaks. The track grew rougher and narrower and Rick began to worry that they wouldn't be able to go much further and he certainly didn't want to reverse back down the mountain.

And then, they saw it.

Rising out of the mountainside as if grown rather than built, the blackened ruins of the McCreedy house loomed. From the first glance, before Rick confirmed it, Diane knew they had found the place from the snuff film.

"That's it!" Rick exclaimed. "That's the tower I saw!"

The tower was pentagonal with four of its sides jutting out over the hillside on a concrete foundation. The walls of the tower were cobbled and blackened at the top where the straight walls crumbled into jutting spires. Diane could easily see why Rick had mistaken it for a gothic castle but in reality they were looking up at the ruin of a luxurious home built sometime in the early part of the century.

"Well, this is as far as we can take the old girl without getting stuck," said Rick, putting the parking brake on.

"I don't expect we'll hold up much traffic here," said Diane. "We haven't passed a single car since turning off. This place is out in the wilderness."

They got out and wandered up the rest of the track until they were standing in the shadows of the ruin. Tangled weeds and ivy cloaked the feet of the tower and a battered wooden door hung on slack hinges. Diane peered into the gloom. It stank in there, an earthy, unhealthy smell.

"Should we fetch a torch, do you think?" Rick asked but Diane was already squeezing inside the doorway.

A spiral staircase wound its way up the inside of the tower and Diane could see light from an open doorway about halfway up. The shaft of light dimly illuminated the walls of the stairway and she could see the markings of crude graffiti; pentagrams, '666' and vulgar inscriptions. The debris that crunched under her feet was made up of broken bottles, pornographic magazines and beer cans.

"Guess the local kids throw the occasional party in here," she said.

Rick didn't answer her as he followed her into the gloom. "Be careful!" he said as she started climbing the stairs.

When she reached the doorway halfway up the tower, Diane found that it opened onto a large courtyard beneath the open sky. Waist-height walls surrounded the area and there was evidence of windows. A stairway on the other side had once led to a now non-existent upper floor.

"This wasn't a courtyard," said Diane. "This must have been an interior room. A dining room or something."

"Or a great hall," said Rick. "This must have been some pile."

He wandered over to the broken wall that looked down over the hillside as it swept away towards Trabuco Canyon. The shadow of the tower loomed over the scrub like an accusatory finger. He looked down at his feet and then back up at the tower. He moved a few paces to the left and then back a little.

"This is definitely it," he said. "This is about where that girl was murdered."

They both looked at the hardpacked dirt floor with distaste and Diane realized that they were both looking for signs of blood. There weren't any.

The place was eerily silent and the confirmation that it was indeed the location of the awful movie made goosebumps ripple up Diane's arms. The isolation of the place meant that truly evil acts could be committed here and nobody would be around to witness them. She wondered how many dark rituals, how many illegal 'snuff films' had been made here.

They wandered from the large room to a series of smaller ones marked out by what remained of their walls. A kitchen was identified by a pair of brick ovens, one of which still had a rusted iron door on it. There was a parlor too, evidenced by the large fireplace and mantle. The purpose of another room was less clear. It was square and had only one door, leading from a short passageway behind the parlor that apparently had no other purpose but to lead to the small room. A single window looked down over the hillside and the drop on this side of the building was far greater than even the side with the tower. The window showed the red-rust streaks of old iron bars.

"I wonder what this place was," said Rick. "Funny sort of room. Some kind of library? Secret sex dungeon?" Diane expected a wink from him at this but his face was entirely without humor. The last twenty-four hours had sapped such amusement from the both of them.

"Wait a minute," said Diane, frowning at the window opening that framed the surrounding hillsides. She reached into her purse and pulled out the polaroid of Christine. Holding it up, she gasped as the broken wall behind Christine matched up with the window opening and it was clear that the distant hills were those same hills in the photograph.

"Oh, God!" Diane moaned. Her knees buckled and she sank down, clutching the polaroid in a shaky grip, her body wracked with tortured anguish.

"What is it?" Rick demanded, hurrying over to hold her. He took the polaroid from her hand and glanced at it.

"She was here," Diane managed. "Christine was here!"

It was like an awful punchline to a bad joke. Diane had always held out hope that this snuff business was a wild goose chase, that it had nothing to do with Christine, that they had found some clue in another case Detective Milton had been looking into. But here was the proof. It was all connected. Christine had been brought here by whoever had taken that picture and then ... What? Murdered in some sick movie like that other poor girl?

She screamed and Rick shook her, his face creased with alarm. She screamed out her frustration and anger that had been building up inside her as they had traveled across the country, stumbling into the dark corner of this sordid world.

"Take it easy, Honey," Rick said. "So she was here! All that proves is that we are on the right track."

"Oh, Rick, don't you see?" Diane wailed. "She was here! She's dead! They killed her! Those disgusting perverts killed her!"

"We don't know that!" said Rick.

"Hey!"

The cry came from the north and Diane and Rick spun around to see a figure approaching them through the ruins. It was a middle-aged man with spectacles and a felt hat.

"What are you people doing here?" he demanded. "Don't you know this is private property?"

"No, I'm sorry," said Rick, getting to his feet and helping Diane up. "We didn't realize we were trespassing."

"Hmm, I figured as much," said the man. "I didn't take you for the kind of freaks who usually break in here."

"You've seen people here?"

"No, not so much *seen*," said the man, a little sheepishly. "Not personally at least, but this place is known for attracting the wrong sort. Who are you two?"

"Rick Margold. This is my wife, Diane. Sorry for snooping about. Is this place yours?"

"No, I'm the neighbor. I live in that house further up the hill. I've never met the owner. He bought the place a couple of years ago and as far as I'm aware, has never visited it. It's a prime location but all this needs to be bulldozed. The sooner the better if you ask me. I heard some hollerin' and saw you both in here so I thought I'd better try and shoo you off. What were you doing in here, anyhow?"

"This photograph brought us here," said Diane, palming away her tears. She quickly tried to compose herself at the sudden appearance of a stranger. She showed him the polaroid. "This is my sister. She's missing. It seems she visited this place."

"It seems she did," said the stranger, inspecting the polaroid. "I haven't seen her I'm afraid but if she's one of the kids that sneaks in here at the dead of night then she's in bad company."

"What do you know about what goes on here?" Rick asked him.

The man puffed his cheeks out and exhaled heavily. "Well, everybody around here has heard of the strange goings on in this place at night. Odd figures coming and going, dressed in black. I've seen the lights myself. Torches. Heard chanting too."

"Chanting?" Rick asked.

"Yeah. That was only the once though, when I was out walking my dog and went past the gate up there. Now, I consider myself a brave man but I'm not stupid. I didn't go blundering in to see what the noise was. No, I headed straight home and turned the lights off, made like I wasn't home. Then, a year ago I found a robe with what looked like blood on it discarded in those bushes over there. There's occult business going on in here, no doubt about it. Satanism, witchcraft, call it what you like but my advice is to give this place a wide berth come sundown. That's when the crazies come out."

"And the police haven't tried to bust them?" Rick asked. Diane noticed that his face had gone pale and waxy.

"Difficult to catch them in the act," the man said. "They only come up here once in a blue moon and when they do you can bet they have lookouts."

"But somebody must know something," said Rick. "These kids will surely be local."

"I'm sure they are but they won't snitch. They've got too good a thing going on here with their sex and drugs. They won't risk blowing it by talking to outsiders. The kids these days, they're out of control. The only one I know who had anything to do with them is Erica's nephew. Old Erica runs the diner down on El Toro Road."

"And her nephew was mixed up with these characters, you say?"

"Well, not exactly mixed up. Mickey's a good kid but he's had his rough patches. Dabbled with drugs just like every other kid these days, it seems. He went to Trabuco High and must have known some of the kids who hang out here. Might even have been one of them, once upon a time, but something scared him off bad."

"Sounds like somebody we'd like to talk to," said Rick, glancing at Diane. "His aunt works at the diner?"

"Sure, you must have passed it on your way up here. Erica's a swell gal, but don't go saying I sent you with stories about her nephew or that's the last slice of key lime pie I'll ever get on the house."

"We'll leave your name out of it," said Rick. "Well, I think we've seen all there is to see here. Thank you for the information, Mister. I guess we'd better head back."

"Didn't mean to yell at you folks earlier," the man said kindly. "You have a good day now, and good luck finding your sister."

By the time they got back to the camper, dusk was starting to settle over the hills, turning them a brilliant orange.

"I guess we could stop in at this diner and see if old Erica is about," said Rick. "It's about diner time anyway and my belly could use a meal."

The diner was a small, well-kept little place tucked in on a bend in the road. There were a few customers and a lady with iron-gray hair scuttled about refilling coffee cups and hollering orders to the chef in the kitchen. Rick and Diane took seats at the counter.

"Be right with you folks," the waitress promised as she brought a stack of dirty plates to the kitchen. As she passed, Diane was able to spot 'Erica' on her name tag.

Rick had spotted it too. *Bingo*, he mouthed to Diane.

They didn't have time to discuss how they were going to grill Erica about the ruins up the hill before she was back to take their order, but Diane gave Rick a cautious look, hoping that he'd remember not to mention the man they had met.

"You folks just passing through?" Erica asked them.

"Yeah," said Rick, looking up from the menu he'd casually picked up. "Just seeing what there is to see up in the hills."

"We found some ruins," said Diane. "Some old house. Looked like there'd been a fire."

"The McCreedy place," said Erica with a nod. "Burned down in 1942 and took old man McCreedy with it. Good riddance to the old bastard, if you'll pardon me."

Diane and Rick stared at her for a moment, thrown off by this sudden turn. They had wanted to ask her about what the local kids got up to in its ruins, not about whoever had owned it originally but the vitriol in her voice made Diane curious.

"Why?" she asked. "What did he do?"

"If you ask folks around here about Alister McCreedy, you'll get no nice answers," Erica replied. "I was just a kid at the time but I heard the rumors even before the fire."

"What rumors?"

"Well, it's not a subject I should go into before you've ordered your food and I'm a little busy but if I can get you both something and you're prepared to wait around until things are a bit quieter, I can fill you in on some sordid local history."

Nodding like a couple of eager schoolchildren at the prospect of a ghost story, Diane and Rick quickly chose a couple of items from the menu and Erica hustled off to relay their orders to the kitchen. Diane had corned beef hash and Rick the chili bowl.

The food was good and the place began to quieten down while they ate. They ordered pie and coffee in order to give Erica as much time as possible to deal with the last of the customers. They finished just as the second to last customer left and Erica sidled over to them, looking as tired as one might expect a middle-aged woman to feel at the end of a long shift.

"Now then," she said. "You two are still here so I guess you're pretty keen to hear about the old McCreedy place."

"Yes please," said Diane.

"Fine." Erica lit a cigarette and pulled an ashtray close. By the way she sucked a drag, Diane could tell this was the first cigarette break she had had in a long time.

"Are you all on your own here?" Diane asked her.

"I am until six. Then Marsha comes in to help with the evening rush. All right then. Alister McCreedy. I hope my cherry pie and coffee lined your stomachs well because this tale ain't for the squeamish. Alister McCreedy was some wealthy type from New England who came here in the 1920s with his wife and baby daughter. He was the one who built that old place up on the hill. There was nothing wrong with him at a glance. A little eccentric perhaps, but a family man with means and reputation.

"It was around about 1940 that the local attitude to McCreedy started to sour. They could never get any help to stay on for very long, you see. The staff all kept quitting and moving away. None of them volunteered anything but when people asked, they just said that they didn't like the kind of things that went on in that house. McCreedy was known for throwing wild parties and had friends from out of town that would come and stay for weeks sometimes. Folks figured it was that which got under the skin of anybody who took work in that house. You know how eccentric rich folks can be. There were whispers of *unchristian* things going on at those parties."

"Do you mean, like, occult things?" Rick asked.

Erica shrugged. "Don't know myself, but it was enough to scare people away. Word got around and after a while the McCreedys couldn't get help for love nor money. They just had to make do, I suppose, the three of them in that big old house. The daughter was homeschooled, so nobody ever saw much of her, poor child. They became quite reclusive and you know how people talk about what they can't see. Rumors snowballed and old Alister became something of the local boogeyman. Turned out he was. I guess the old rumor mill gets it right once in a while. You see, the ugliest part about the whole thing is that ever since McCreedy had come to these parts, children had started to disappear."

"Disappear?" Diane asked, her eyes wide.

"Not that it was all blamed on McCreedy at first, you understand," Erica said. She snuffed out the butt of her cigarette in the ashtray. "But after what they found out about him, it's not hard to look back and see things in a different light. Kids go missing, they always have, and sometimes without a trace. Maybe some of the kids who vanished around here would have vanished anyway but when you start getting ten, twelve, fifteen kids vanishing from the same small community, you know that something doesn't add up. You know that there's something rotten in your neighborhood."

"McCreedy," said Rick.

"Yep," Erica replied with a decisive nod. "It took a while for folks to put two and two together, of course, but suspicions were running rampant. My own friend was one of the missing. Sandra. Dear Sandra. We were the same age and we used to walk home from school together every day. One march I got sick with scarlet fever and was home from school for a while. That's when Sandra went missing. Just up and vanished into thin air without a trace. Accusations were already beginning to fly at McCreedy and it only took a couple more similar disappearances before the fire happened, accident or otherwise."

"You mean there were suspicions of arson?" asked Diane.

"Plenty of suspicion but nothing conclusive. But after what was discovered in the burnt ruins came to light, few people were interested in finding out, including the police. They had enough of a job on their hands."

"What was found?"

"Bones. In the great big fireplace. *Children's* bones."

"Jesus," said Rick.

Alister and his wife died in the blaze but their twelve-year-old daughter was taken out alive and rushed to hospital. Word has it that she lived and was fostered by some family somewhere. As for the old McCreedy house, it fell into a ruin and there it sits; a black stain on this community and something we all try and forget."

"Some folks we spoke to today say that local kids like to hang out there at night," said Rick.

"'Hang out' ain't exactly how I'd put it," said Erica. "And it's not just kids from what I've heard. There's some sort of cult that has laid claim to the place. Whether they were influenced by Alister McCreedy or his disciples or his fan club, I've no idea, but they've been seen on the property, sneaking about in robes and lighting torches, that kind of thing. Drug-fueled orgies, according to my nephew Mickey."

"Is he involved?" Diane asked, glad that Erica had finally mentioned her nephew.

"No, he ain't. He might not be the smartest tool in the shed but he ain't stupid. They tried to get him to join and I do believe he went along to one of their meetings but something scared him so bad he didn't want nothing to do with them after that. They even threatened him but he told them to go take a running jump. And when a kid like my sister's Mickey gets squeamish about something, you know it's gotta be something goddamn awful."

"Erica, do you think it would be possible for us to talk to your nephew?" Diane asked.

Erica frowned. "What for?"

"Well, we're not just here on vacation. We're trying to find out what's really going on up at the McCreedy house."

"You're not from the papers are you? I won't have my nephew's name – *our name* – connected to all this."

"No, we're not from the papers. This is personal. My sister, you see, she went missing and we know that she visited the McCreedy house recently. Possibly in the company of the very people who threatened your nephew."

Erica remained unconvinced and Diane pulled out the well-worn polaroid to show her. Erica's eyes flitted over it and she seemed to be mentally wrestling with something.

"Well, I don't know what our Mickey could tell you that I haven't already."

"Please," said Diane. "We think my sister is in grave danger. If she's part of all this then we want to pull her out. Bring her back home. If there's anything your nephew could tell us then it might be helpful."

"All right then," Erica said at last. "I'll speak to my sister. Mickey ain't got a job and he sits around on his fat ass most days so I'm sure he'll have the time to talk to you. Whether or not he'll have the inclination to talk is another matter. Those creeps scared him pretty good."

"We understand," said Diane. "And we'd really appreciate it."

"Don't mention it," said Erica, softening up a little. "I know what it's like to have someone close vanish. I just pray your sister didn't meet the same fate as my friend Sandra."

CHAPTER 9

Erica's nephew agreed to talk with Rick and Diane two days later. They had camped in O'Neill Park and were preparing to set out when a police car from the Sheriff's Department rolled into a vacant spot opposite theirs. Rick froze and watched the driver's door open and the figure of Detective Garrett climb out. He spotted Rick and affected a friendly smile as he ambled over.

"Glad I found you folks," he said. "You were just about to head out, huh?"

"Yeah," said Rick, trying to inject a little innocent confidence into his voice. "Moving on, y'know. What brings you here, detective?"

"Well, you do, as a matter of fact. You and your wife, that is. I've been looking for you and you've led me quite the chase."

"Chase?" Rick tried to keep any hint of panic out of his voice. Had they found the murder weapon? Had they somehow tied it to him?

"Just a figure of speech, Mr. Margold. "You folks sure do like to move around."

"Well, yes, we're still looking for my wife's sister."

"Of course, of course. Any luck?"

"Not exactly."

"Been all over, huh?"

"Not exactly all over. But here and there."

Rick felt like he was being pumped somehow. What was this guy getting at? If he was here to arrest him then he was taking his sweet time about it.

"Been out of the county?"

Careful, Rick thought. The last thing he needed was this detective knowing that he'd been down to San Diego to watch a goddamned snuff movie. That was a whole different barrel of trouble.

"No, just stuck around Orange County," he lied. "Camping grounds mostly. Cheaper than motels."

"Camping grounds, right. That's what I wanted to talk to you about in fact. Is uh, is your wife around? I'd like to talk to you both."

"Sure." Rick rapped on the camper door. "Honey? Come out here for a sec."

Diane came down the steps.

"Detective Garrett!" she exclaimed. "What a pleasant surprise!"

"Not a coincidence, I'm afraid," Garrett replied. "I've had our boys calling around all the camping grounds for a sign of you. Caught up with you at last!"

"Have you found out something about my sister?" Diane asked.

"Ah, no, that's not why I'm here."

"Then why are you here, detective?" Rick asked. He was getting fed up with all this beating around the bush.

"Did you stay at the San Juan Campground on the night of the 15th?

Jesus Christ, thought Rick. *He knows something ...*

"Yes, we did," Diane answered before Rick could think of anything to say.

"Were you disturbed by anything during the night? Any noises or trouble of any kind?"

"No," said Rick, perhaps a little too quickly. "Slept like logs. Very peaceful spot."

"Yeah, I guess it is," Garrett replied. "The thing is, three teenagers were murdered on that stretch of road not ten yards from the campground."

"Oh my god!" Diane exclaimed.

And in that moment, Rick was proud of his decision not to tell her anything about that night. Her reaction was genuine, just as he had planned for in this eventuality. Now he had to make sure his own was up to scratch.

"You're kidding," he said. "Murdered!"

"Yeah, ugly scene. Hacked up with an axe in the back of their van."

"It seemed such a pleasant, peaceful place," Diane said. "I can't believe it ..."

"Of course, we're interested in talking to everybody who was camping there that night, see if anybody saw anything or heard any noises. But there's a reason I wanted to talk to you both in particular. These three kids, God rest their souls, drove a blue Dodge van with a custom paint job. Did you happen to see this vehicle on the road on your way down?"

Rick found his face frozen in a rictus half-smile. The conversation was moving too fast. Should he confirm or deny? Either choice had its pitfalls ...

"Did it have a wizard on the side?" Diane asked.

"Yes, Ma'am, it did."

"Oh my God, is that why you're here? You think my husband had something to do with their murders?"

Jesus, Diane!

"Oh, no, Mrs. Margold, why on earth would I think that?"

"Well, we did encounter them on the Ortega Highway as a matter of fact. They tried to run us off the road. I don't know what their problem was but they seemed to see it as a bit of sport. We were terrified."

"But you got away from them."

"Yes."

"And that's the last you had to do with them?"

"Well. We pulled into a roadhouse and then so did they. My husband ... uh, he bawled them out and they took off. And that's the last we saw of them."

"Bawled them out?" Garrett repeated. "Hmm. Not quite how I heard it."

"What did you hear, detective?" Rick managed, his voice a little hoarse.

"The way the witnesses tell it is that you threatened their lives."

"Oh, come on now, Detective Garrett!" said Diane with a short laugh. "It was just a figure of speech! We were nearly killed by those kids and my husband let off a little steam, that was all!"

"How come you didn't mention this to me when we met? It couldn't have happened twenty-four hours before you came into the Sheriff's Department."

"Well, we were planning on calling the police from that roadhouse but then they came into the parking lot and after my husband's altercation with them, they just seemed kind of scared off. We didn't think much more of it, just kids out for kicks. Dangerous kicks of course, but, well, you know kids."

"Sounds like you scared them pretty bad, Mr. Margold."

"Well, they damn near killed us!" Rick protested. "Busted up my ladder pretty good! I had a right to be mad at them, don't you think? But that's a far cry from actually wishing them harm!"

"I know, I know," said Garrett, putting on a little kindness at last. "You're not actually a suspect, Mr. Margold, but I just needed to hear your side of the story. Is what your wife just told me accurate?"

"Yeah. That's how it happened. I may have flown off the handle, I'll admit, but I wouldn't wish that on anybody. I mean, Jesus, those kids didn't deserve that."

"Well, somebody thought otherwise. And between you and me, those kids weren't angels. From what you've told me about their stunt on the highway and from what we've found out about them, well, let's just say they were asking for trouble."

"But even so ..." said Diane.

"Oh, sure, I know. Awful thing. And until their killer is caught, I'd recommend you keep your door locked at night."

"We will," said Diane.

"Where are you off to next?"

"Oh, we'll be staying here for the foreseeable future. We have an appointment in El Toro with somebody who might know something about my sister."

"You've been quite the detective duo," Garrett said with a smile. "Been all over the county asking questions, huh? I know how that goes."

"Well, now that we're back from San Diego, we hope to stay put here for a while."

"San Diego?"

Rick grimaced and tried not to show it. *A couple of sentences ago would have been a great time to stop talking, Honey,* he thought.

"Yeah, we chased a lead down there a couple of days ago. Somebody knew somebody, that kind of thing. The telephone number of that smut peddler you turned up at the scene of Mr. Milton's suicide helped us a great deal."

"Well, I think we've used up enough of Detective Garrett's time today, Honey," said Rick, keen to nip this interesting conversation in the bud. He knew Diane wouldn't actually tell Garrett about the snuff movie but she was dancing awfully close to it.

"I'm glad we could help you in some capacity," said the detective. "And your husband's right, I do have a lot on my plate today. Got a killer to catch, you understand. Take care now."

"Goodbye, detective," Diane said.

They watched the detective stroll back to his car and roll it down the avenue of parked campers until it turned right and vanished.

Rick exhaled a sigh of relief. They had just about made it. He felt his armpit. The swelling hadn't got any better and it now throbbed with the stress of the whole situation. He felt woozy and light-headed and desperately wanted a drink. But it was only ten in the morning for Christ's sakes. Was he developing a drinking problem? Well, if he was, who could blame him?

"Rick!" Diane cried from around the back of the camper. "Come over here!"

"What is it?" he said. "Has that fucking ladder come loose?"

"Just get over here!"

There was a note of fear in her voice and as he rounded the corner of the camper, he understood why.

"What the hell is that?" Diane cried in alarm, her finger pointed at a small, red symbol that seemed to have been painted on the back of the camper above the left tail light. It was two 'V's crossing each other with a line through the both of them. Little circles punctuated the end of each line.

"Search me," said Rick. "Looks like some sort of occult symbol. Jesus, has somebody hexed us?"

Diane reached out a finger to smear the greasy-looking substance.

"Don't touch it!"

"What's with you, Rick? Don't tell me you're starting to believe in this occult crap? It's only lipstick."

"Lipstick?"

"Yeah. And I know whose. Recognize the shade?"

"Should I?"

"She was sitting close enough to you."

"Oh, you don't mean ..."

"Yeah. Brenda left us with a little parting gift."

"You mean that thing has been on the camper the whole time? While we went to San Diego and back?"

"I knew that bitch was mixed up in all this somehow. You remember how she tried to persuade us not to go to San Diego? She was probably sent by this cult to throw us off track. We're lucky silly little curses are all she's capable of."

"I can't believe she'd curse us. Maybe it's some sort of protection sigil."

Diane gave him a look that suggested she couldn't believe he was defending her.

"It's just that she struck me as more of a white witch than a satanist or what have you. It could be that she wanted to ward off evil in her own peculiar way."

"Whatever it is, I want it off our camper."

Rick signed and set to work, fetching a bucket of soapy water. He succeeded in washing off most of the lipstick but a faint pinkish residue still remained. It would have to do or they would be late for their appointment with Erica's nephew.

CHAPTER 10

Mickey Kelsey and his mother lived in a run-down farmhouse off El Toro Road as it veered north-east away from the town. Empty fields flooded the view on both sides of the road, devoid of other houses or any sign of habitation.

Mickey's mom was a tired-eyed woman pushing fifty with an untidy tangle of hair hanging down on either side of her ruddy cheeks. She was in the process of lighting a cigarette as she opened the door to them and gazed at Rick and Diane with weary eyes behind tinted glasses. She sucked a drag and blew it out the corner of her mouth.

"You'll be the folks wanting to speak with Mickey," she said. "Come on in, then."

The house was shambolic. Junk was piled in every corner and the tv set was blaring *Wheel of Fortune* through a fug of cigarette smoke.

"He's down in the basement," Mrs. Kelsey said. "Never comes up, most days."

A plank door in the recesses of the home opened onto a rickety staircase that led down into the basement where heavy metal music throbbed. An unshaded bulb illuminated the Led Zeppelin and Black Sabbath posters which were plastered to the whitewashed walls.

Mickey was an overweight nineteen-year-old in a tight black t-shirt and flared jeans. He wore his hair long and his general look and taste in music gave Rick an uncomfortable reminder of the three dead teenagers.

"Mickey?" Diane asked the youth as he scrambled off the worn-out sofa that, along with the unmade bed, a shabby side table and some shelves fashioned from breeze blocks and planks, was the only item of furniture.

"Yeah? You the folks my auntie told me about, huh?"

"I'm Diane and this is my husband, Rick."

"Cool."

"We understand you know something about the kids who hang out up at the old McCreedy place some nights."

"Yeah, well, I can't really tell you too much about them. They're dangerous and they don't take too kindly to people talking about them."

He was a polite, mild-mannered kid but clearly nervous. He didn't seem too bright, but Rick saw that as a positive. They could get him to spill what he knew, if he wasn't too scared that is.

"We'd be grateful for whatever you could tell us, Mickey," Diane said, putting on her best sympathetic schoolteacher voice. "Do you mind if we sit down?"

"Sure, knock yourselves out."

Mickey flopped back down onto the sofa and they sat down beside him, Diane next to him and Rick next to its worn arm. The seat sunk down alarmingly beneath him and he felt a spring digging into his ass.

"When did you first make their acquaintance?" Diane asked.

"In my junior year," Mickey replied. "A buddy of mine, Jeff Mason was into all that occult stuff. I was at a party with him and he started talking about it all, about the sex and the drugs and the cool rituals they did."

"What kind of rituals?"

"Well, the way he explained it was that if there was something you really wanted, or if there was somebody who was your enemy and you wanted them out of the way, then you could conduct a ritual to make sure it happened. But that was all personal stuff. You had to vow yourself to Satan first and that was what this group he was a part of did in the ruins of the McCreedy house. We were into the same stuff, Jeff and me, and he asked if I was interested in getting involved. It all sounded pretty cool so I said yes.

"We met on a Saturday night. Jeff and I went alone. He made me put on a blindfold before we entered the ruins. There were a bunch of people already there but I couldn't see them, only hear their voices chanting. They were waiting for me. Somebody – not Jeff – told me to take off my clothes. I didn't want to, but the man asked me if I truly wanted to be Satan's disciple. I was so scared. I wanted to leave but I didn't know how I could get out of it. So I took my clothes off ..."

They gave him a moment. He was visibly upset just thinking about this stuff.

"What happened next, Mickey?" Diane asked.

"They told me to kneel and repeat some words. I can't remember exactly what they were but it was all about giving my soul over to Satan and working evil in his name. Then, a cup was pressed to my lips and I was told to drink. I did and nearly threw up. I don't know what was in that cup but it was lukewarm, thick and tasted like metal."

"Blood?" Rick suggested. "Did they make you drink blood?"

"Could be," Mickey replied. "At least, that's what I think it was. I drank it all, forced it down, trying not to spew. And then my blindfold was removed. I was surrounded by people wearing robes. I couldn't see their faces beneath their hoods. It was then that I noticed that three others were kneeling naked with me; two boys and a girl. They looked just as sick and terrified as I felt."

"Fellow initiates," said Diane.

"Yeah, well, we weren't actually initiates. At least not yet. That night was just the first trial."

"There were others?" asked Diane.

"Yeah. But more stuff happened on the first night. Stuff I don't really wanna go into because it's all kind of embarrassing. I don't know if I was drugged or something but I did stuff that I wouldn't normally have done."

"Like what?" Rick asked.

"Sexual stuff," Mickey said, his face coloring. "We all started fucking, and I don't remember how it started. Us four new kids and then the guys in robes, they were naked beneath them. It turned into one big orgy.

"Was anybody filming this?" Rick asked.

"Filming?" Mickey said, his eyes wide. "Jesus, I hope not! Why do you ask?"

"No reason. I mean, did this group ever talk about making movies. Porno, that kind of thing?"

"Not that I can recall. They might be involved in that stuff but I didn't get in too deep with them. Jeff drove me home after that night. We didn't speak. I couldn't believe what he'd gotten me into. I was scared but the truth is, I was kinda thrilled too. It was the most exciting thing that had ever happened to me."

"So you stuck with them?" Diane asked. "You didn't go to the police?"

"How could I? What would I tell them? 'Excuse me, officer, I had sex with a bunch of people up in the mountains as part of some satanic rite and they made me drink blood'? I'd get laughed at or maybe even locked up. I didn't know how weird this thing got or what other stuff they were involved with. Like, where did they get the blood? Whose was it? I didn't want to implicate myself in anything."

"Wise move," said Rick.

"Did you ever meet up with the group again?" asked Diane.

"Only once," said Mickey. "It was to be the second part of my initiation; the bit that would see me fully inducted into the group. We met up like before and I was blindfolded again. I thought maybe the other initiates would be there but when they took my blindfold off, I found myself alone in a circle of robed figures. They dragged a dog in front of me, a German Shepherd. They put a knife in my hand and told me I had to kill it."

"Kill the dog?" Diane asked, appalled.

"They held it down for me. It was muzzled and knew something was up. I don't know where they got it. Maybe it belonged to one of them or maybe they snatched it. It was so pathetic, so scared ..." Tears welled up in Mickey's eyes at the memory.

"Why did they want you to kill a dog?" Rick asked.

"They sacrifice dogs in their rituals," said Mickey. "Offer them up to Satan."

"Why dogs?"

"I don't know."

"Go on, Mickey," Diane urged.

"I had the knife in my hand," the boy continued. "They told me to put the blade to the animal's throat and pull it quickly across. They said that was the kindest way to do it, so that it bled out quickly. I just wanted to leave, man, I didn't want nothing to do with the group anymore. I just wanted to go home but I knew they wouldn't let me. I was scared of what they might do to me if I refused. So I ... I did it."

"Killed the dog?"

"Yeah, I cut its throat like they told me and they collected its blood in a chalice. Then they all took their robes off and passed the chalice around. They started smearing the blood on their bodies. They poured some over me. It was warm and sticky but I just kept looking down at that dog as it died, the foam bubbling at the gash I had opened in its neck, its eyes wide and frightened. I watched it die as they all started fucking around me, rubbing the dog's blood all over each other."

He stopped and the silence hummed like a void as he began to sob. Rick felt ill. He wanted to get out of that damned basement, out of that house and breathe the fresh air. The images of the snuff film forced themselves to the forefront of his mind: the visual accompaniment to Mickey's words. He remembered how they had rubbed the blood of the dead girl on every inch of naked skin in their sick orgy in those same ruins. There was no way it wasn't the same group.

Mickey recovered himself somewhat with the aid of Diane's kind words and a Kleenex from her handbag. "When I got home, I spewed in the shower," he said. "I watched the vomit and dog's blood swirl down the drain and I swore that I would have nothing more to do with the group. I never went back and I stopped talking to Jeff."

"Was it so easy to leave, knowing what you know about them?" Diane asked.

"They tried to get me to come back. Tried to scare me."

"How?"

"Jeff tried at first. Kept calling me up and stopping by, telling me that I couldn't quit or they'd get angry. I told him to fuck off, that I wasn't interested in this shit if it involved killing dogs. The next day, I found the head of a German Shepherd in our front yard. I don't know if it was the head of the one I killed. It was too bloodied and fly eaten. I got rid of it before my mom saw it. I didn't hear anything else from them after that but the message was pretty clear though. I couldn't go to the police without implicating myself. They were guilty of nothing I wasn't. So I kept my mouth shut. Until now."

"Mickey, do you know if this group still meets in those ruins?" Diane asked him.

"As far as I know."

"They haven't moved on somewhere else?"

"No, they wouldn't want to. They get a big kick out of it, doing all these rituals on the grounds of the McCreedy house."

"The site has some special significance to the group?" asked Diane.

"Sure. You heard all about Alister McCreedy, right?"

"Yeah, your aunt told us all about him but what I mean is, this group conducts its rituals in the ruins of the McCreedy house because it's important to them and not just an isolated creepy location?"

"Yeah, they know all about McCreedy and the stuff he was into. Some of the older guys knew McCreedy way back."

"Really? You're sure about this?"

"That's what they told me. One old guy said he used to partake in the rituals McCreedy used to hold up at the house."

"What sort of rituals?"

"He didn't go into it, but he saw McCreedy like some kind of messiah, really! He was nuts about the guy."

"Do you have any names of anybody in the cult that we can speak with?"

"No way, man!" Mickey said, suddenly alarmed that he had nearly been coaxed into saying too much. "I never saw anybody's faces during the rituals, so I could never identify anybody to the police even if I wanted to. But I met some of them at parties Jeff took me to and I knew they were involved. Not everybody there was part of the cult but some were and it was always like a nudge and a wink, y'know? Even if I did know some names, I wouldn't tell you. They'd kill me! Don't you get what I've been saying? This group is serious. They're not just kids fucking around with pentagrams."

"I know, Mickey, I know," Diane said. "We wouldn't do anything that would get you into trouble. What about this Jeff Mason boy? You said you went to school together."

"He moved away. About a year ago. I don't know if he's still involved – he may have tried to distance himself from it all like I did. Lives in L.A., I think. I lost contact with him, so I'm not sure."

"All right. Well, thank you, Mickey, you've been really helpful."

"Yeah? You won't go around saying that I've been talking to you?"

"No, we'll keep our conversation confidential, I promise."

"OK, then. Uh, I hope you find your sister."

"Thank you, Mickey."

They went back upstairs and said goodbye to Mickey's mom who was still watching *Wheel of Fortune*.

The bright sunlight and fresh air was a welcome relief after the dim, smoky Kelsey house and the grimness of the tale Mickey had just told them. Rick breathed the air deeply and fought down the urge to vomit.

"Are you OK?" Diane asked.

"Yeah, just need a minute," he said. Once his nausea had subsided, he straightened. "Well, I can't say that was all that helpful," he said. "That kid doesn't seem to know much and even if he did he might not tell us. He seems scared half to death."

"I know. But I think he told us the truth. Luckily for him he wasn't fully initiated into the cult. If he was then he'd surely know more about them. A group like that must keep themselves pretty secret from outsiders."

"What now?"

"I'm going back to the library in El Toro."

"The library?" Rick asked. "Why?"

"I need to find out all I can about Alister McCreedy. Don't you see, Rick? This cult is somehow connected to him and I want to find out how."

"I don't see how this will help us find Christine."

"You got any more leads I don't know about?"

"No," Rick admitted, sheepishly.

"Then this is the best way forward that I can think of. If we can understand this cult then we might understand how Christine got involved with them and hopefully, where she might be now."

CHAPTER 11

Rick still felt woozy driving into town and, as they parked outside the library, he said to Diane; "Look, Honey, I don't feel up to more cult research, especially not in a stuffy library. Do you mind if I stay put for this one?"

"No, that's fine. I'm more than at home in libraries and you'd only be hovering over my shoulder."

She took her bag and her notepad and headed towards the library. Rick sat back in his seat and closed his eyes. He felt awful and he knew that it wasn't just the gut-churning tale of satanic ritual and animal sacrifice they had just been subjected to. He felt his forehead and withdrew his hand quickly. He was burning with a fever. His armpit was agony and he carefully caressed the large swelling there. When would this damn thing start to go down? It was definitely larger than it had been this morning. Maybe it wouldn't go down. Maybe it had to be lanced or squeezed or something. Was he to expect some sort of eruption of pus at some point?

He slowly got up and made his way to the bathroom. He needed to take a look at this thing. The sight that greeted him as he pulled off his shirt in front of the mirror sickened and horrified him.

The armpit was almost wholly filled by a bulging orb of flesh, unnaturally red with inflammation. His armpit hair was splayed out in all directions and there was one unusually thick and wiry hair in the center of the swelling. Rick wiggled it with his finger. It looked out of place, like it wasn't one of his own hairs. Was this what was causing the swelling? Some sort of infected follicle or overly thick hair that had worked its way through his skin?

He seized it between his thumb and forefinger and braced himself as he made to give it a yank. This was going to hurt like hell, but he was determined to remove the cause of his pain.

He pulled hard but instead of agonizing pain and a burst of pus, the hair spooled out of its follicle in one long streamer with little to no resistance. He kept on pulling it until it came free and held it up, gazing at it in appalled horror. He had pulled a strand of black, wiry hair from his armpit about a foot in length. It dangled from between his thumb and finger, wet and shiny like something pulled from a shower drain.

Disgusted, he tossed it in the trash and inspected his armpit. A small, inflamed follicle remained, its deep hole showing where the hair had been nestled. How long had that thing been growing inside his armpit? He shuddered to think of it coiling round and around like a ball of black string. Perhaps now that the vile object had been removed, the swelling would start to go down.

He gave the lump a tentative squeeze and ground his teeth in pain. No pus came and he resigned himself to letting it take care of itself. Maybe he could hurry it along with some antibiotics? There had to be a drug store somewhere in this town and he was still keen for fresh air. He needed to get his fever down in any case.

He got out of the camper and started walking towards what looked to be the most fruitful end of town. Stores and small businesses lined the street. He passed a bar called Pitt's and found his gaze drawn to its dingy interior with its low lights over billiard tables and glinting bottles of booze on mirrored shelves. He could do with a quick pick-me-up. It was after lunchtime after all. But no, first the drug store. Then he would reward himself with a drink.

Pleased with his resilience, he carried on past Pitt's and eventually found a drug store. The clerk was a pain in the ass and kept asking him questions about what it was for and how severe it was. Rick didn't feel like going into intimate detail and he certainly didn't want to mention the long strand of hair he had pulled from his armpit. The man eventually caved to Rick's stubbornness and sold him a box of antibiotics that promised to clear up most infections including swollen lymph nodes. He also sold him some painkillers and suggested warm compresses. Rick thanked him and hustled out of the store.

He popped the pills on the street, first the antibiotic and then a painkiller. Then he headed back the way he had come, his heart set on a drink to take the edge off the day. Mixing booze and antibiotics was probably not a good idea. He knew the back of the box of antibiotics would warn against it but those warning labels covered everything but the kitchen sink. If you followed those to the letter, you wouldn't do anything but sit in a darkened room and he was on vacation, for Christ's sake. He deserved a little R&R.

Pitt's was typical of a small town barroom. It had a couple of billiard tables, some booths for quiet conversation and a long bar where a friendly barkeep kept himself busy. There weren't too many customers at this time of day and Rick relished the quiet, relaxed atmosphere of red leather, green felt, oak paneling and cool beer.

"New in town?" the barkeep asked as he scraped the foam off the top of Rick's beer.

"Vacation," Rick said. "Staying up at O'Neill Park."

"Nice place. Family?"

"Just the wife and I."

He took the beer and swallowed a gulp. *Boy, that hit the spot.*

"The newspaper archives are in the basement," said Frank the librarian. "We've started putting them on microfilm, but we've only got as far as the mid-sixties I'm afraid. If it's the fire of '42 you're interested in, we'll have to get our fingers grubby the old-fashioned way."

Diane smiled as she followed Frank down the stairs into the library's basement. He was a likeable man and seemed eager to help her even though he must surely be wondering what interest some New Yorker on vacation had for Alister McCreedy and his house on the hill.

The newspapers were bound in heavy leather tomes and Frank dug out the local ones for 1942 and carried them over to a study table, flicking on the overhead lamp. After rifling through the yellowed pages for a while, they eventually found a mention of the fire. It was such a short piece considering that it was a local newspaper reporting on the death of two prominent figures of the community.

"It's almost just a footnote," Diane said. "Like they were reluctant to report on it."

"Well, McCreedy wasn't a popular man around here," said Frank. "Maybe some out of town papers give a better picture."

He fetched her the volumes for some of the larger papers and after more searching, they found a longer piece in the *Oakland Tribune* which even included a picture of McCreedy and his family. The photograph was under the headline; 'Family man and wife slain in horrific Orange County fire'. The *Tribune*, it seemed, was willing to go into more detail than the local papers but the article shed no light on whether or not arson was suspected. It did reveal one new detail; the name of the McCreedy's twelve-year-old daughter, Persephone.

"The child survived and was fostered?" Diane asked Frank.

"I did hear something to that effect," said Frank. "Some family out of state, is what I heard. Poor kid. Although the fire probably did her a favor. It can't have been much fun growing up in that household."

"Do you believe that it was arson?" Diane asked him.

Frank shrugged. "That's what the grapevine says, even if the papers don't. As I said, he wasn't a popular man."

Diane squinted at the black and white picture through the lens of the reader. After hearing so much about Alister McCreedy and the dark rumors surrounding him, it was strange to finally look upon the man. He was a stern-faced fellow with a thin moustache and glasses that seemed to reflect just enough of the camera's flash to obscure the true nature of his eyes. She tried to see something in them, some hint at the evil mind within, but she knew it was useless. If her career as a historian had taught her anything, it was that photographs were little more than droplets of time, frozen forever. Sometimes they told you a great deal, sometimes they told you nothing at all. Context was everything. *Who were you really, Alister McCreedy?* she wondered. *Is what they say about you true or were you an innocent man, the victim of small-town slander?*

And what of Mrs. McCreedy and little Persephone? Rachael McCreedy looked the dutiful wife, hair immaculately curled, gaze distant, as if she were not really there. But it was the face of little Persephone that really moved Diane. The picture couldn't have been taken long before the fire for the girl looked around eleven or twelve. Her hair was dark and held back in tight pigtails. There was no happiness in that face and Diane shared some of Frank's sentiment. What had that poor kid suffered in that house? And whatever became of her?

"You seem pretty interested in this whole affair," Frank said. "It's not just about architecture, is it?"

"No," said Diane, sitting back in her chair. She rubbed her strained eyes wearily. "I'm sorry, Frank, I wasn't quite telling you the truth. It's nothing to do with architecture. It's my sister, you see. She moved out here a few months ago and I think she's gotten involved with some sort of cult in this area."

"Cult?" asked Frank, his face showing some alarm.

"I'm afraid so. They meet up in the ruins of the McCreedy house and perform awful rituals to Satan."

"Who told you this?"

"I didn't believe it at first, but we spoke to a local kid who was hooked up with them at one point. He was able to get out, but the things they made him do ... And now my sister might be held against her will by those cretins."

She took the polaroid of Christine out of her purse and showed it to Frank. He looked at it sympathetically but said nothing.

"I doubt she'd have popped in here to do a little research," said Diane, "but it was worth a shot."

"I'm afraid I haven't seen her," said Frank as he handed the polaroid back to Diane. "But why all this interest in Alister McCreedy? These devil worshippers are probably just attracted to his name and the rumors surrounding him."

"Well, our informant seemed to think that some of the cultists knew McCreedy back in the 1940s. They were his disciples or something. Did he really run some sort of cult or was it just wild parties?"

"Well, I don't know about cults," said Frank, "but old McCreedy was definitely into the *occult*. Dark stuff too. We have a book of his in this very library."

Diane blinked and straightened in her seat. "Alister McCreedy wrote a book on the occult?"

"Sure did. Can't think of the name off the top of my head. Something 'Working'. It was a book of magical rites he claimed to have performed. Baloney, of course, but I took a peek inside it once and the bit I read made me keen to never look inside it again."

"Frank, I must see this book."

"Well, all right. If you insist. Just make sure you take it all with a dose of salt. McCreedy was a loon and more than one person has tumbled down the rabbit hole reading up on this trash."

Diane followed him upstairs and waited patiently while he riffled through the card catalogues. "McCreedy ... McCreedy," he muttered under his breath as he flipped through the cards. "Ah! Here we go. Alister McCreedy. *The Chorazin Working With Commentary and Other Papers*. I knew it was something like that. Now, let's see ..." He plucked a small notepad and a pencil from the breast pocket of his shirt and winked at Diane as he flipped it open. "Memory's not what it used to be. If I don't write down the number, I'll forget it before I'm halfway over there."

He shuffled off towards the bookshelves and Diane followed in his wake as they made their way down the aisles. "Here's all the occult stuff in the Philosophy and Psychology section. Hmm ..." he ran his finger down the shelf as he inspected the titles. "Not seeing it. How about you?"

"No," said Diane as she scanned the titles on witchcraft, astrology and tarot cards. "Maybe somebody checked it out?"

"Well, that would be alarming to say the least," said Frank. "Follow me."

They went over to the main desk and, after some investigating Frank concluded, with some embarrassment, that the book seemed to have gone missing.

"It was checked out over a year ago," he said. "By a 'Miss Rachael Buse'. She has received several notices from us that the book was overdue but has not responded. There's a note here that the telephone number provided is disused. Well, that is disappointing, I must say. But these rare volumes are tempting targets for unscrupulous types."

"Does Miss Rachel Buse live locally?" Diane asked.

Frank frowned over the rims of his glasses at her as librarians have a habit of doing. "Please don't go knocking on doors asking about our library books. I shouldn't have told you her name at all. An overstep on my part."

"Oh, I wouldn't dream of it," Diane lied. "But I do have to wonder what somebody would want with McCreedy's book unless they are part of this little group of 'disciples'."

"Yes, I'm inclined to agree," said Frank. "Well, she gave us a local address but, if the phone number is discontinued, then I am tempted to think she has moved on. We can look her up in the White Pages and see if she has a new address."

They checked and found nothing local.

"Could be that she married or moved out of state," said Frank.

"Very well," said Diane.

"I'm sorry I couldn't be of more help," said Frank.

"That's all right. I have a few more things I'd like to look up in the newspaper index if that's OK?"

"You go right ahead."

"My husband is meeting me for dinner soon, so I won't be too much longer."

She headed back down to the basement and began looking through the index cards of local newspapers for any articles about the occult. If there really was a satanic cult operating out of El Toro or Trabuco Canyon and it had been doing so for thirty-odd years, then there was a chance they had slipped up somehow and some rumors had got into the press.

Her belly was rumbling and she was wondering where Rick had got to by the time she came across an article in a 1952 issue of the *Orange County Reporter* with the headline; 'Nanny flees after shocking exposure! Bizarre occult rites performed on infant.'

What the hell have I found now? Diane wondered as she squinted through the viewer at the newsprint.

'*A nanny working for a prominent Newport Beach family fled authorities last night amid accusations of impropriety and the endangerment and exploitation of a child.*

The Lane family, who live in a large home overlooking the maritime industries of Newport Beach, had employed twenty-two-year-old Rachael Buse to work for them as a nanny for their two-year-old son. On the evening of May 1st, Mrs. Lane walked in on Miss Buse who appeared to be conducting some sort of occult ritual. It is understood that the child had been drugged and blood had been taken by Miss Buse who was immediately dismissed.

Rachael Buse had been living with the Lanes for almost six months and is believed to have been practicing some form of witchcraft involving the young Lane child. Mr. Lane, a businessman of some standing in the community, called the police but, upon their arrival at the Lane residence, it was discovered that Miss. Buse had escaped from a second-floor window. Her current whereabouts is unknown.'

Diane was gobsmacked. Rachael Buse ... the very woman who had stolen Alister McCreedy's book from the library a little over a year ago! Who the hell was this woman who had been lurking around since the 1950s? Had these 'bizarre occult rites' performed on the Lane child in 1952 been something to do with McCreedy's scene? Whoever this woman was, she was still alive, had been in the area recently and was still interested in the occult.

"I don't blame her, how could I?" Rick said, before taking a gulp of his second beer. "Some things just aren't meant to be. But I know she thinks I do, no matter how many times I've tried to tell her that it's OK. You got any kids?"

"Boy and a girl," said the barman as he served another customer who had taken up his perch at the other end of the bar.

The place had livened up a little as evening approached. As well as the man at the bar, a young couple were playing pool.

"Lucky man," Rick told the barman. "We can't even talk about it anymore. She just gets upset. I don't know why she can't just move on. *I've* accepted it. Kids would have been great but it was never on the cards for us. It's better to focus on something else and not let that hole in your life get bigger and bigger. You gotta keep moving, you know? That's why we bought the Winnebago. Jesus, talk about a band aid for a relationship! We've taken that thing across the whole country and not spent one day of it on a proper vacation. It's all about her kid sister. She's gone missing, you see?"

The barman nodded in silent sympathy. Rick knew he was blabbering on but it felt like it had been ages since he had spoken to anybody but Diane. The barman was a good sort and seemed to be used to drunks pouring their hearts out to him.

Jesus, is that what I've become? Rick wondered. *A miserable drunk telling his woes to a barman?*

He looked at his watch. It was past five. Time had really flown by and Diane would probably be finished at the library, wondering where he was. He paid his tab, got up and left the bar.

He felt light-headed as he stepped out onto the street. His gut churned as the cool beer no doubt played havoc with the antibiotics but he felt refreshed. He no longer burned with fever and the pain in his armpit was tolerable thanks to the combination of painkillers and beer.

The shadows were long on the sidewalk and, as he crossed the street that cut across El Toro Road, he spotted a couple of men that seemed to be dragging a young woman between them. She had her back to him, and he couldn't see her face. She was either drunk or sick as her legs barely seemed to be working. The men pulled her roughly towards a tan station wagon.

Rick stopped and stared, wondering if he should intervene. The scene looked sinister but, as he ran through alternate situations through his mind, he realized that he might get a fist in his face or worse if he stuck his nose in. The kid might be a younger sister who had got tanked and was now being dragged home. Or she might be a prostitute being manhandled by her pimps and if *that* was the case, he'd best mind his own business.

But there was something about the girl that kept him staring after her. She was blonde and wore a floral top and pink hotpants. Just like Christine did in the polaroid.

Startled into action by this revelation, Rick hurried down the street towards the altercation. The men had succeeded in wrangling the girl into the back of the station wagon and one of them was getting into the driver's seat.

"Hey! Wait!" Rick cried as the driver gunned the engine and, wheels spinning, the station wagon pulled out onto the road.

Rick caught a glimpse of the girl's face through the rear window, masked through tangled curls of blonde hair. He couldn't be sure it was Christine but it looked damn near like her.

The station wagon roared off down the street and Rick jogged to a stop, his lungs heaving and his armpit throbbing with the exertion. He squinted and tried to make out a license plate but the car had gained too much distance. He watched impotently as it turned a corner and vanished.

CHAPTER 12

"Where the hell have you been?" Diane asked as she saw Rick jogging towards her. She had left the library over half an hour ago and had been anxiously waiting for Rick, wondering where he had wandered off to.

"I went to the drug store," Rick said dismissively. "But Diane! Christine is here! Here in El Toro! She's here!"

Diane's face paled. "Where?"

"Two guys were manhandling her into a car just a block from here. I chased after them, but they got away before I could get their license plate."

"Are you sure it was her?"

"Well, I mean, I'm pretty sure."

"You saw her face?"

"No, not exactly, but she was wearing the identical outfit to what she's wearing in that polaroid!"

Diane covered her mouth with her hand, willing it to be true and not another false lead.

"She's here, Diane," Rick said. "And she's alive."

They drove around for the rest of the evening until it got dark, looking for the tan station wagon. El Toro was a small town and they managed to drive down every street twice but there was no sign of either the car or Christine. Dejected although still infused with optimism, they headed back to O'Neill Park, stopping for dinner along the way.

"I'm going back to the library tomorrow," said Diane as they got ready for bed. "If you drop me off, you can take the camper and continue looking for that station wagon."

"You bet," said Rick. "You still keen on finding out more about this cult, huh? Find out anything yet?"

"You won't believe it but I've found the name of one of McCreedy's possible disciples. He wrote a book you see. And a local woman checked it out and never returned it. She was involved with some occult stuff in the 1950s in Newport. Tried to do some occult ritual on a child but was chased off."

"And she's living around here?"

"Maybe," Diane said. "Frank – that's the librarian who's been helping me – thinks she's moved on. Her phone number is disused but I want to find out where she lives and go pay her a visit."

Detective Garrett spat the mouthful of lukewarm coffee back into the Styrofoam cup and set it down on the edge of his desk. *Damn you, Halloran,* he thought. *Is it too much to ask that you keep a fresh pot on?* He would pick up some decent coffee when he headed out.

It had been a trying night. Not only was his sister-in-law still on at him to take on her wayward son and put the fear of the law into him, but he was making little progress on the slain teenagers case or how it connected to the Hillary and Munroe murders. All he knew was that they *were* connected.

He was still trying to figure the Margold people, knowing that they fit into it all somewhere. It was a hell of a coincidence that the husband had roughed up the Marston kid shortly before he and his two friends were found murdered a stone's throw from where the Margolds had camped for the night. It wasn't enough to bring him in on but there were definitely pieces missing in the story.

And there was something about Rick Margold that seemed, well, *off.* Garrett had seen enough guilty mugs in his time to recognize one when he saw it. And Rick

Margold had looked positively sick with guilt when he had approached them in O'Neill Park. He had been sweaty-faced and shifty, looking like he wanted to be anywhere else. And then he had lied to Garrett about their having been in San Diego. The wife didn't seem to think it was important but then why would the husband lie? What had they been up to down there?

The phone rang and he grabbed for the receiver, nearly knocking over the cup of cold coffee. "Garrett," he said into the receiver.

"Detective Garrett, this is Detective Dobson of the NYPD,"

"Good to hear from you, Dobson."

"I thought you'd like to know that I ran a check on these Margold birds. Zip on the broad. Born Diane Fenniston in Brooklyn Heights. Not so much as a parking ticket but there's some juice on her hubby, Richard Margold."

"Do tell."

"Nothing heavy but he ran into some trouble in middle school. Was brought in after beating some kid half to death in the school parking lot. He was charged with assault but nothing ever came of it. The word was that he was picked on by a group of boys and he really let one of 'em have it. The thing is, he was only thirteen. The kid he pummeled was sixteen."

"Must have really lost it," said Garrett. He tried to match up the image of a feral and raging thirteen-year-old with the shifty but mild-mannered Richard Margold he had met twice in the past week and found it a struggle.

"That's not all," Dobson said.

"Oh?"

"When he was twenty-one, he was brought in for questioning about the murder of a man in an alleyway in Queens. He was seen leaving the scene, but we couldn't pin anything on him. Didn't seem to know anything about it but let's just say there were some holes in his story. Whatever you're trying to pin on this guy, I'd say he was a sure bet. A violent past is always a giveaway."

"You think Margold killed this guy?"

"No proof but we don't believe in coincidences in this line of work, do we?"

No, we don't, Garrett thought. *Especially not where Richard Margold is concerned.* There were too many coincidences surrounding that guy by half. "Thank you for your help, Detective," he said to Dobson.

"Any time. You boys making headway with that satanic cult business? I hear some kids got hacked up recently."

"Yeah," said Garrett.

"You can always bet that when it comes to cult activity, there are kids involved. Drugs too. We got freaks on our streets here in New York that would give Charlie Manson nightmares. It's always worse in the hot summers. There's no limit to their depravity. You got any suspects in mind?"

"One or two," Garrett said.

"Good luck with 'em."

"Thanks."

He hung up and looked down at his notepad where he had jotted down the gist of Rick Margold's colorful past. *So, Richie-boy, you have a violent streak.* You wouldn't think it to look at him. But then, some of the most depraved bastards are good at hiding their true natures. *And if this is what you're hiding, Richie-boy, what other secrets have you got?*

Halloran stuck his head in through the doorway. "Just got a call from a residence on El Toro," he said. "Suicide but might be something else. You wanna come along?"

"Something else?" Garrett asked.

"Yeah, some kid blew his brains out in his mom's basement. Anderson's over there now and he said something about it not adding up."

"Jesus, not another murder!" Garrett said as he got up and followed Anderson out to his car.

The house was in El Toro, within spitting distance of O'Neill Park, Garrett noted with grim interest. *What have you been up to now, Richie-boy?* He wondered.

"Getting a sense of déjà vu?" Anderson asked Garrett as he went down into the basement to look at the dead body.

"Don't let the sheriff hear you say it, but yeah, I am," Garrett replied.

It was a small room dimly lit by an unshielded bulb that was still swinging about after the photographer had knocked it, sending the shadows leaping dizzyingly across the walls. The deceased lay in the fetal position on the floor of what had been his bedroom, what was left of his head curled in towards his chest. The rest of his head was spattered against the heavy metal posters on the wall behind the bed. The mother was still wailing in the living room above their heads and the subterranean lair had the chthonic feel of Hell.

"The pistol is registered to him," said Deputy Maidstone as he climbed down the stairs, holding the bloodied revolver in its evidence bag. "The mother doesn't seem to know anything about it so I guess he kept it to himself."

"Maybe he felt the need of some protection," said Garrett.

"He likely sat on the edge of the bed when he blew his brains out," said Deputy Maidstone, squatting down by the corpse. "Then the force of the gunshot hurled him back onto the bed and he bounced right off. At least that's how we figured it."

"Now where have I heard that before?" Garrett said. "What did you get out of the mother? Has this kid any enemies?"

"Well, the neighbors say that he was a bit of a recluse. Kept to himself and stayed in his basement mostly. The mother did say he had some visitors not two days ago. A married couple came here to ask him questions about some sort of cult."

"A cult?" Garrett asked. "That sounds promising. Who were these people?"

"Well, the mother didn't catch their names. She said they were from New York and pulled up here in a Winnebago."

Garrett's mouth opened in surprise and his cigarette nearly fell out. "Bingo!" he exclaimed.

"What?" said the deputy, looking up at him with some confusion.

But Garrett was already halfway up the stairs. He pushed his way past the photographer and went out to his car. Grabbing the radio microphone, he called the dispatcher at the Sheriff's Department. "Karen, that you? Garrett here."

"It's me, Detective," the voice on the other end squawked.

"Listen, Karen, I want you to put out an APB on a 1976 Winnebago Chieftain."

CHAPTER 13

They headed to the library, first thing after breakfast.

"I'm going to distract Frank for a little while," Diane told Rick. "I want to look up a few things in any case. While he's helping me, I want you to go behind the desk and find the ledger where the library's membership information is kept. It's a black book with red corners. Find out where Rachael Buse lived. With any luck she'll still be there."

"Sure thing," said Rick.

They were both looking out the windows at every parked car on their way down into El Toro, keeping their eyes peeled for the tan station wagon. It was like looking for a needle in a haystack and even if they did spot one, there was no way of knowing if it was the same car Rick had spotted the day before. They'd probably have better luck pursuing the Rachael Buse angle.

"Hi, Frank," said Diane as they entered the library. "This is my husband, Rick."

"Please to meet you," said Frank, shaking Rick's hand. "I just opened up. You folks are early. More newspapers to go through?"

"Oh, we couldn't sleep," said Diane. "Not after all we found out yesterday. I wanted to read up a little on whatever it was Alister McCreedy was writing. Chorazin something?"

"The Chorazin Working," said Frank.

"Yeah, does that mean anything to you or is it just occult gobbledygook?"

"Well," said Frank, running his fingers through his thinning gray hair, "most occult stuff has some basis in either history, religion or alchemy, even if it does get perverted into looney stuff. Chorazin sounds biblical. We might start there."

"Great. Could you give me a hand?"

"Sure."

As they headed over to the card catalogues, Rick hung back and Diane motioned to the desk with her eyes. He nodded and slunk off.

After some research, Diane and Frank found out that Chorazin was an ancient village on the northern shore of the Sea of Galilee. According to the gospels of Matthew and Luke, it was one of three cursed cities condemned by Jesus along with Bethsaida and Capernaum for their refusal to repent from their wicked ways.

"Apparently," read Frank, "there is mention of these three cities in later non-canonical scripture relating to the apocalypse."

They dug deeper and, in a book on New Testament apocrypha, they found an excerpt taken from the *Apocalypse of Pseudo-Methodius* written in seventh century northern Syria.

"Listen to this," said Diane, reading from the book. "... the Son of Perdition will appear. He will be born in *Chorazaim*, nourished in Bethsaida, and reign in Capharnaum. Chorazaim will rejoice because he was born in her, and Capharnaum because he will have reigned in her. For this reason in the third Gospel the Lord gave the following statement: 'Woe to you Chorazaim, woe to you Bethsaida, and to you Capharnaum - if you have risen up to heaven, you will descend even to hell." She looked up from the book at Frank. "*Son of Perdition*? My Sunday school lessons are failing me ..."

"It's a vague term used a couple of times in scripture," said Frank with a grim face. "Generally it refers to two people, firstly Judas for his betrayal of Christ and secondly, the Antichrist."

"My god," Diane gasped. "Is that what all this is about? Is that what McCreedy wrote a book about?"

"It appears so," said Frank. "The Chorazin Working, taken at face value, seems to be an attempt to manifest the Antichrist."

Rick cleared his throat behind them, making Diane jump. "Sorry to disrupt your research," he said. "But Diane and I have … an appointment?" He made eyes at Diane and she understood. He has the address.

They left the library and got into the Winnebago. Diane's nerves were all over the place. Not only were they potentially about to come face to face with somebody who was deep into the cult that had abducted Christine, but the things she had found out about McCreedy's occult interests made her sick to her stomach.

"They're trying to summon forth the Antichrist," she said to Rick as he pulled out of the parking lot.

"What?"

"This cult. McCreedy. Rachael Buse. All of them. They're all trying to start the apocalypse or something. That's what Frank and I found out. Chorazin is supposedly the birthplace of the Antichrist."

"Well what's all that got to do with snuff movies and abducting Christine?" Rick asked.

"I don't know," Diane said. "This all seems to get worse and worse the further into it we get."

The address was a house on Los Alisos Boulevard. The woman who opened the door had never heard of Rachael Buse and claimed that the previous owner had been an elderly man called Mr. Hargreaves. In the background they could hear kids screaming and playing. This was a family home and Rachael Buse wasn't here. As Diane and Rick walked back to their Winnebago, Diane couldn't help but express her frustration.

"Just when I think we're getting close to the head of this thing, we run into a dead end," she said. "Christine is here somewhere but always just out of reach."

"I'm guessing that whoever has her has made them-selves scarce," said Rick. "Like this Buse woman."

"You don't look too good, Honey. Are you feeling all right?"

"No, not really. I've got some blasted summer cold. Picked up some pills at the drugstore but they don't seem to be doing the trick."

They spent the rest of the day driving around the outskirts of El Toro, extending their search for the station wagon. They spotted some on the road and one parked in somebody's driveway but none of them had anything suspicious about them. Their frustration built as the hopelessness of their task began to set in.

"We should head back to the library," said Diane. "There must be some way of tracking down the elusive Miss. Buse, wherever she has moved to. It beats driving around and around looking for some non-descript vehicle."

"You bet," said Rick.

As they turned back onto the main road leading into El Toro, they passed an abandoned farm building on the other side. A tall silo towered over the overgrown land, its rusted domed roof collapsed in on itself against the slowly deepening dusk.

"Just a minute," said Rick as he glanced out the driver's window at the derelict property. He slowed down and jabbed a finger at the rundown buildings. "What does that look like to you, jutting out from be-hind that old barn?"

Diane squinted and followed his pointed finger. "A vehicle half hidden in the bushes," she said. "It looks like the rear end of ..."

"A tan station wagon," Rick finished for her.

He pulled over and they gazed across the road at the property and the car which had been run into the foliage that grew thick at the rear.

"Is it the same one?" Diane said.

"Sure looks like it," said Rick. "C'mon, lets take a looksee."

They got out and crossed the road. A dirt track led through the abandoned buildings and was shaded by the tall, curving trees that whispered gently in the afternoon air on both sides. The buildings up ahead were dark and ominous with small black windows that seemed to peep at them.

Someone had made an attempt to hide the car. It lay half sunken in a ditch to the side of the largest building. It was a tan station wagon, all right. There was a blanket on the back seat and a balled-up mess of duct tape in the footwell.

"I have an ugly feeling about this," said Diane.

"Yeah, this is the car," said Rick. "I've no doubt. Looked like they kept Christine bound up. Maybe they were moving her from one place to another. Maybe they heard about us asking around and got spooked."

"Do you think ...?" Diane began, gazing up at the ruined buildings with their flaking paint and broken windows.

"That they've got her in there?" said Rick. "Could be. Could be we've found her, Honey."

Diane felt a chill of excitement and also trepidation. What Rick said could be true and they might be within hailing distance of her little sister. But part of her dreaded what they might find. What if the cult *had* got spooked? What if they had taken Christine away and ... well, got rid of her for good?

"This might be it," said Rick. "Wish I owned a gun."

"Wait, Rick," Diane said, grabbing him by the arm as he made to head up the path towards the largest building. "We can't go in there, not us, not right now."

"What are you talking about?" Rick said. "We might have found her, Diane! We might have found your sister! Of course we have to go in there!"

"It's a cult, Rick, they're dangerous! We don't know how many of them might be in there. We know that these people have killed before and they won't think twice about getting rid of us."

"Jesus, Diane, I didn't think you'd chicken out at the last minute, you of all people ..."

"I'm not chickening out!" she snapped. "We just need to be smart about this or risk putting ourselves and Christine in danger. Now here's what we're going to do. We're going to drive back into town and we're going to call Detective Garrett and tell him everything."

"The cops!" Rick exclaimed. "Oh, come on, Diane! When have the cops been interested in any of this?"

"Garrett is one of the good ones, Rick, I know he is. He'll help us when we tell him what we've found out about this cult operating in his backyard. This isn't just a missing persons case anymore."

Rick sighed. "Fine. I just don't like wasting precious seconds, that's all."

They crept back to the Winnebago and quietly drove on, hoping they hadn't aroused the suspicion of anybody in the abandoned farm.

They drove into town and looked for a payphone. As they passed the library, Diane saw that the lights were still on.

"Looks like Frank hasn't clocked off yet," she said. "I bet he'd let us use his phone."

They parked and hurried over to the library. Frank was putting books back on shelves when they found him in the fiction section.

"I was just about to close up," he said. "Technically we *are* closed."

"I know, I'm sorry, Frank," Diane said. "But we think we've found my sister."

Frank put the stack of books down on the little trolley. "You're kidding?" he said. "That's great!"

"We need to use your phone, is that OK? It's time we involved the police."

"The police?" Frank said. "I thought they were involved already?"

"They've been next to useless so far, but I'm going to tell them what we know about this cult. I know they have her, Frank. I know they have her at an abandoned farmhouse on the edge of town."

"Well, the phone out back is out of order, I'm afraid," said Frank. "Damn company are supposed to send someone but it's been three days ..."

"Well, there must be a payphone somewhere," said Diane. She turned to Rick. "What about that drugstore down the street?"

"Yeah, they have one," Rick said. "I'll go, Honey. You stay here with Frank."

"But ..." Diane began.

Rick was already pushing the double doors open. "I won't be long!"

"Well," said Frank. "I guess we'll hold the fort here. Coffee?"

"I thought you were just about to close up," said Diane. "I'm so sorry to be a bother ..."

"No bother! I usually stick around after closing up anyway. Plenty to do here and I always make a pot for myself. Make yourself comfortable. I'll be right back."

Diane sat down at one of the reading tables in the center of the library while Frank vanished into the librarian's office. She drummed her fingers on the tabletop in agitation. She should have gone with Rick. It was better than sitting around here doing nothing.

Frank returned with a pot of coffee and two mugs. He poured out the coffee and sat down opposite Diane.

"While we wait," he said, "how about we resume the hunt for the elusive Rachael Buse?"

"Well, we know for certain that she doesn't live at Los Alisos Boulevard," said Diane. "I have a confession to make about that. We paid the house a visit earlier today. Sorry."

Frank frowned. "Well, I guess it doesn't matter much. You are looking for your lost sister, after all. You didn't mention the library book?"

"No."

"Good. Look, why don't I fetch some directories and we can start going through them. We'll begin with Southern California and then go on from there."

"All right," said Diane, cheered a little by the prospect of doing something.

Frank headed off and came back with a trolly groaning with telephone directories. As he passed the topmost one to Diane, Rick pushed his way through the doors.

"You spoke to Garrett?" Diane asked.

"Yeah," said Rick. "He wants to head out there now. I'm going to meet him at the property."

"I'm coming too," said Diane, making to get up.

"No!" said Rick. "It's too dangerous. We don't know what we might find there. Garrett is bringing backup and it might get ugly."

"Rick ..." Diane protested.

"Do this for me, Diane, please. Besides, it looks like you're back on the case here." He nodded at the stack of telephone directories.

"We're trying to track down our mysterious book thief," said Frank. "It's best if you stay here, Diane. Let the police do their job. We've got a full pot of coffee and plenty of directories to go through."

Diane reluctantly said nothing.

"I'll come right back here as soon as I know anything," said Rick.

He headed back out and Frank followed him to lock up. Diane sat down. She reached for the hefty tome Frank had put down on the table for her and pulled it towards her.

"That's the spirit," said Frank, returning. "There are some things we can't control and in those cases it's best to keep your head down in a book, that's what I always say."

Diane smiled half-heartedly at his attempt to cheer her up. But perhaps he was right. With any luck, everything would be all right and Christine would be safe in her arms before the end of the night. She hadn't given much thought to what would happen then but now that she had the time to think on it, she realized that even getting Christine back would not be the end of it. She wanted to do whatever she could to stop this evil cult from abducting more girls, from taking more innocent lives in their sick movies. Christine would undoubtedly be a big help in telling the police all she knew but Diane knew a few things too and if she could root out the head of this vile serpent, she was determined to be instrumental in cutting it off.

Renewed by a heated desire for revenge, she applied herself with vigor, finishing the volume Frank had given her and fetching another from the cart. Frank grinned and kept pace with her. They carried on like this for a while and Frank topped up their coffee cups. Between them they had covered most of Southern California and Diane was heartened with the knowledge that if Rachael Buse was in any of these directories, then they would eventually close in on her, even if it took the whole night.

Somebody banged on the library doors and made them both jump. Was Rick back so soon? Diane's heart fluttered with hope. But it wasn't Rick. It was a man holding something up to the glass; a wallet with a detective's gold shield for their inspection.

"Garrett!" said Diane.

"Police, open up!" Garrett said.

Looking concerned, Frank went over to let him in. "What can we do for you, Officer?" he said. "It's late and we're closed up."

Garrett ignored him. "Mrs. Margold?" he said, approaching the table. "Where is your husband?"

"My husband?" Diane said in confusion. "He's gone out to meet you."

"What?"

"You agreed to meet Rick at the farm on Los Alisos Boulevard."

"I have no idea what you're talking about, Mrs. Margold."

"Then you didn't speak to him on the phone? My husband didn't call you tonight?"

"No, he did not. We're here to talk to you and your husband regarding the suspected murder of a boy over on El Toro Road."

Diane's heart froze. "What boy?"

"He apparently committed suicide by blowing his brains out, although we don't figure it played out like that."

"Was it Mickey ..?

"He died in a very similar fashion to the private detective you hired to look for your missing sister."

"*Was* it Mickey?"

"Yes. It was.

"Oh, God!"

"You and your husband visited him a couple of days ago. His mother says you were talking to him about cults and Satan and stuff. There's a whole lot of bad business going on in this county and everywhere I turn I seem to run into you and your husband. Now, I want to know what the hell is going on and where your husband is!"

"He's gone to an old, abandoned farm on Los Alisos Boulevard," said Diane. "We think my sister is being held there. There is a cult. They have been committing murders across the county. We've been trying to track them down, to find my sister. That's why our paths keep crossing. The cult killed Mickey because he talked to us! We didn't have anything to do with his murder, but we have his blood on our hands anyway! If we hadn't made him talk, if I hadn't ..."

Garrett ground his teeth in frustration. "A cult? Committing murders? And when were you planning on notifying the police about this?"

"I thought we had notified you tonight, Detective. My husband said he called you. He went out to meet you at the farm to bring Christine back. He must have gone alone ..."

Garrett growled. "I know the place. You stay right here."

He headed for the doors and Diane watched him go with dread clawing at her heart.

Goddamn it, Rick, she thought. *What the hell are you playing at?*

CHAPTER 14

Rick parked the Winnebago and looked up at the abandoned farm buildings that lay spread out like debris, silverish in the moonlight.

He had lied to Diane. He hadn't called Garrett. No way. Tell that damned detective everything? Diane had lost sight of the bigger picture. She had forgotten that they had paid to watch a snuff movie. *He* had paid to watch a snuff movie. More than that. Garrett suspected his involvement in the murder of the three teenagers. Thanks to Diane, Garrett knew he had lied about going to San Diego and he wasn't about to let Garrett pick up any more clues by joining up with him.

No, he would do this alone. If Christine was here, he would get her out. He would end this thing once and for all and then they could be on their way back to New York, leaving this whole nightmare behind them.

His armpit throbbed and he clutched it, screwing his face up in pain. Goddamn it, what was this thing? Why wouldn't it go away? As his fingers explored the lump beneath his shirt, he felt something hard there. Something foreign.

He got up and went into the bathroom compartment and unbuttoned his shirt. Examining his inflamed armpit in the mirror, he could see something small, white and shiny nestled in the center of the lump from where he had pulled that long strand of black hair.

What the hell ...?

He fingered it and clenched his teeth at the pain. It was hard and smooth like a small stone or bit of grit. How had that got in there? He had the uneasy feeling that it had come from inside his body and was being slowly pushed to the surface.

Gasping with pain, he began working it out with his fingernail. He dug and squeezed as he uncovered more and more of the dark lump. The pain was unbearable but he had to get this thing out of him!

At last, it came free and he held it up to the light, his fingers slick with his own blood. When he realized what it was, he gave out a cry of disgust and the object tumbled from his fingers to rattle around in the sink before disappearing down the plughole. It was a tooth. A human tooth. But not, he realized, an adult tooth. Rather, it was the milk tooth of a child.

What the fuck?

He fumbled in the medicine cabinet for some gauze and bandage. His armpit wasn't bleeding profusely but there was an ugly hole from where he had plucked the tooth. Covering it with gauze, he wound the bandage around his shoulder. *Please God let that be the end of it!*

He felt like he was going mad. First hair and now fucking teeth? What was happening to him? It was all like some crazy nightmare.

Focus, Rick. Stay on mission. He was here to bring Christine home. There would be time to examine his own physical and mental health afterwards. All that mattered now was getting Christine back so they could head home.

He fetched a flashlight from the glove compartment and got out of the Winnebago, sucking the night air deep into his lungs to ease his nausea and cool his jumping nerves.

There were no lights showing in any of the windows of either the farmhouse or any of the outbuildings. Perhaps the place truly was abandoned. Perhaps Christine wasn't here after all.

Only one way to find out.

Flicking the flashlight on, he headed up the path towards the barn. He would check that first.

A length of rusty chain was used to secure the rotten doors but there was no lock. Grabbing one end of the chain, Rick pulled it free and swung open one of the doors which creaked noisily, before stepping in.

The place was falling apart and hadn't been used in many years. He shone his light up and down the cavernous room, illuminating rotting hay bales and disused farm equipment, rusty with age. Thick cobwebs clogged the corners.

Nothing here.

He left the barn and poked around in some of the other outbuildings. They were in a similar state as the barn and contained nothing of interest.

The house then.

The porch steps creaked as he climbed up onto the gallery that ran around the house. The ripped screen door hung on one hinge and the solid door behind it was locked. Rick crept around to one of the large windows at the rear of the property. One was already broken, and he did his best to remove the larger shards of glass before attempting entry. He clambered up onto the sill and pushed his way through the musty, tattered curtains to fall heavily on the bare floorboards of what had once been a living room.

Expecting to have alerted the cult to his presence by his clumsy entrance, he lay flat and frozen for a few heartbeats. Silence reigned throughout the house. He got up and moved into the hallway. The sweeping beam of his flashlight illuminated strips of peeling wallpaper and faded patches on the floorboards where furniture had once stood.

The kitchen had been largely ripped out although there was an empty beer can standing all alone on a windowsill. Left behind by the last removal worker to leave the house? Or evidence of current habitation?

Trying to make the floorboards creak as little as possible, Rick headed for the stairs and began to climb them, slowly. He found several bedrooms leading off from the landing, each of them empty, and a bathroom stripped of its tiles. After fully investigating the top floor, Rick stood on the landing and peered out of the smashed window that looked down on the overgrown lawn below. He cursed in frustration. There was nobody here. Christine, if she had been brought here at all, was long gone.

He had been so sure he could end it all tonight. Now he would have to go back to Diane and tell her that the hunt was still on. His hopes of returning to New York tomorrow, back to his old life, back to normality, evaporated in the moonlight.

"Don't break out the champagne yet," said Frank, not looking up from the phone directory he was currently studying. "But I may have found our book thief."

"Where?" Diane asked, getting up and hurrying around to his side of the table. After nearly an hour of scouring the directories, her index finger was sore and her eyes funny.

"22 Selva Drive, Veblum Springs," he replied. "Now where the heck is that? Newport Beach, somewhere. Let me get a map."

A folding map of Southern California revealed that Veblum Springs was a small town in the hills above Crystal Cove. It wasn't close to anything but hiking trails and an old road that Frank claimed had fallen out of heavy use at least twenty years ago.

"She really wanted to hide from the world, didn't she?" Frank said.

Somebody rattled the doors and they both looked over to see Rick bathed in the light through the glass.

"He's back!" Diane said. "But where's Garrett?"

Frank went to let him in.

"What happened?" Diane asked.

"It was a bust," said Rick. "No Christine. No anybody, in fact. That place hasn't seen any activity for a long time. I figure they just chose it as a handy spot to ditch the car."

"What the hell is going on, Rick?" Diane snapped. "Garrett was here, looking for you."

"Garrett?" said Rick. "Aw, hell, why didn't he meet me at the house like we agreed?"

"Don't lie to me, Rick! I know you never called him!"

Frank coughed nervously and shuffled off to his office mumbling something about having some books to stamp. Diane regarded Rick expectantly.

He sighed. "Look, Honey, I'm sorry I lied to you. But we couldn't bring Garrett into this, not now! You know what we've done in pursuing this. What I had to go through down in San Diego."

"So you went off to tackle this cult on your own like John Wayne? Rick, the police should know what's going on in Orange County!"

"And they will! As soon as we get Christine back, we can make all the phone calls we need to to get these scumbags put behind bars. But you gotta see things properly, Diane. I committed a crime when I paid to see that damned movie. I don't want to have to explain that to Garrett or any other cop when we don't have a bigger fish to throw them."

"I don't get you, Rick, I just don't," said Diane. "You've been acting so differently lately, so secretive. We are in over our heads with this cult, when are you going to realize that? You remember that Mickey kid?

Garrett came here and told me that somebody blew his brains out. Just like they did to Ed Milton."

"You're kidding!"

"No, I'm not kidding, Rick! This cult knows we're on to them! They're covering their tracks!"

"Exactly! You think I don't know how dangerous they are! What makes you think we can trust the cops even? Aw, hell!" he kicked a chair savagely. "What's the use, anyway? Christine wasn't there so we're back to square one!"

"Well, not quite," said Diane.

He eyed her, picking up on a tone of excitement in her voice that her anger at him couldn't quite conceal. "What?" he asked. "What have you found?"

"The home address of Rachael Buse."

"Are you sure it's her?"

"Well, we haven't come across any others with that name in Southern California so it's a pretty good bet. She's living in some one-horse town in the hills about fifteen miles south-west of here."

"You wanna go check it out?"

"There's plenty of camping grounds in those hills. I say we head out in the morning and see if we can't pay our little cultist nanny a visit."

"I say we go tonight."

"Tonight? Why?"

"These people, Diane. They're like spiders with their webs. We've made enough of a racket snooping around. If we wait, then this Rachael might be given a warning and move on before we can catch her. Let's drive down there now and we'll get her first thing in the morning."

"Ahem," said Frank at the doorway to his office. "I couldn't help but overhear that you're planning on heading out. You'll need this." He held up the folding map. He had circled Veblum Springs with a red circle.

"Thank you, Frank," Diane said. "You've been a wonderful help. We'll be out of your hair now so you can finally shut up shop."

"Well, I just hope you find your little sister," said Frank. "I wish you the best of luck. Oh, and if you happen to come across the missing book, I'd greatly appreciate it if you returned it to us."

Rick and Diane headed out into the streetlights of the parking lot. They got into the Winnebago and Rick slid into the driver's seat and reached up a hand to adjust the rear-view mirror. He found himself looking up into a hideous pair of eyes, blazing with a furious hate right back at him. He spun around in his seat, terrified of what he might find looking over his shoulder but there was nothing there.

He looked back at the mirror and saw only his own, tired eyes, ringed with dark circles and set in a pale, sweating face.

Keep it together, Rick, he thought. *We're so close. Don't lose it now.*

"You OK, Rick?" Diane asked.

"Yeah, yeah," he replied. "Just fine."

He turned the key in the ignition and they rolled out of the parking lot and onto the highway heading south-west.

Garrett awoke to a blinding headache. At first, he blamed it on the bright morning sunlight streaming in through the windows. Did he have a hangover? Jesus, how much had he put away last night? Then he realized that he had no idea where he was.

As his eyes adjusted to the brightness, he was able to focus on the layout of the sparse room he found himself in. Somebody got up and hurried out and he caught the flash of a nurse's uniform.

Hospital.

And then the events of the previous night began to organize themselves in his brain. Yeah, he was in hospital. That figured.

He remembered leaving the library and hightailing it to the abandoned farm on Los Alisos. He had found the Margold's Winnebago there and saw a flashlight moving about in one of the upper rooms of the derelict house. He considered calling for backup but ultimately decided to proceed and see if he couldn't talk Rick Margold into taking a trip down to the station to straighten a few things out. He drew his gun, just in case.

The door was locked, leaving Garrett to wonder just how Margold had got in. He hammered on the flakey woodwork and identified himself. No sound came from within and he took a few steps backwards to gaze up at the upper bedrooms. There was no light up there now.

"Margold!" he yelled. "It's Garrett! I'm coming in! Just want to ask you a few questions!"

When that yielded no answer, he booted the old door in and stepped into the gloom.

Switching on his own flashlight, he made a sweep of the ground floor and then made his way up the creaking staircase to the upper floor.

"Margold?" he called out again. "I'm not in the mood for games. Just show your face and we can talk this out, man to man."

He stood on the landing and looked up and down it. Several doors were closed and Margold could be hiding behind any one of them. Now he really wished he had waited for backup.

He walked towards the large window at the end of the hallway, his pistol gripped in his sweaty palm. There was a loud creak and at first he thought it was the floorboards beneath him but then realized – too late – that it was the sound of one of the doors behind him opening.

He spun around and was unable to get a shot off at his attacker as a body slammed into his and pushed him with a staggering force backwards. Garrett was no featherweight but he found himself driven towards the tall window at his back. His feet backpedaled despite his effort to negate the seemingly superhuman strength that was pitted against him.

As the glass shattered behind him and he tumbled through the air, he caught a glimpse of Rick Margold's face framed in the broken window above him, his eyes blazing with a hideous evil Garrett had not thought physically possible in the face of a human being. There was something beyond human about those eyes and they were the last things he saw before he hit the ground and all went black.

The nurse came in with the doctor and Garrett was given a thorough going over. His arm was bandaged and he had sticking plaster in various spots around his body, including his face.

"You are lucky to be alive, Mr. Garrett," said the doctor once he had completed shining a light in his eyes. "A fall from such a height could have killed you or given you irreparable brain damage. Fortunately, the overgrown garden cushioned the impact somewhat. Can you remember anything about the incident?"

"Enough to go after the son-of-a-bitch who pushed me," said Garrett. "How long have I been out?"

"About twelve hours," the doctor replied. "Your partner, Mr. Anderson was here and the sheriff has been notified of your condition."

"Where is Anderson?"

"He was called away."

Garrett tried to get up.

"Oh, no," Mr. Garrett!" the doctor said. "You need to take it easy. I have more tests to run."

"Well, you'd better hurry up and do them, Doc," said Garrett. "Because I need to get the word out about a dangerous criminal. Where's your phone?"

"We will bring you an extension if you need to make an emergency call," said the doctor.

The nurse fetched him a glass of water while a hospital porter brought through a telephone and set it on the nightstand. Garrett called Anderson and told him what had happened and that the Margold couple had to be brought in as soon as possible.

Once the doctor had finished his tests and found nothing of concern besides a mild case of concussion, Garrett argued and threatened and ultimately convinced them to discharge him. Wincing at the wounds from which shards of glass had been plucked, he got up, got himself dressed and headed down to the parking lot where a cab stood waiting to take him to the Sheriff's Department.

As Garrett crossed the asphalt towards the cab, a second car revved its engine and came hurtling towards him. Still groggy from being out of the game for twelve hours, Garrett barely had time to register the danger and it was only due to the shout of warning from the cab driver that he saw the other car bearing down on him.

He flung himself between two parked cars as the car roared past in a squeal of tires, continuing through the parking lot and out onto the road before vanishing.

"You get that license plate?" Garrett yelled at the cab driver who hurried over to help him to his feet.

"Hell, no!" said the cab driver. "I was too busy covering my eyes against seeing you flattened!"

Garrett stood and stared in the direction the car had taken. Blood had begun to seep from his wounds which had been reopened during his sudden burst of action. He ignored the jarring pain.

So, he thought. *There's more than one crazy bastard who wants me out of the way. What the hell is going on?*

Well, he was going to find out, damn it! And there was one more thing he had decided upon. He would call his sister-in-law and tell him that he would take on her no-good kid. If somebody like Rick Margold was running around murdering teenagers then he was damn sure going to do whatever he could to protect his nephew.

Chapter 15

The hotel stood against the dark desert hills, the lights from its windows at once inviting and yet somehow foreboding.

It looked like it had been built in the early years of the century in the Mediterranean Revival style. Spanish arches, stuccoed walls and wrought-iron balconies made it look like a giant mission house left to decay in the mountains. It wasn't a ruin for it clearly enjoyed some periodical upkeep, but time had taken its toll on the old dame of a building, leaving its red-tiled roofs grimy, and its white paint flakey. Some of the larger exposed patches revealed that the building had once been painted pink.

"Well," said Rick. "22 Selva Drive. This is the place."

"I wasn't expecting a hotel," said Diane as they sat in the Winnebago and peered at the building from across the road. "Why was it listed as a residential address in the White Pages?"

"Perhaps Rachael Buse is the owner," said Rick. "What a place for a hotel, though! Still in business too by the looks of it."

"I guess we could book a room," said Diane. "I don't know what we might find in there, but I feel a hotel is preferable to sleeping out in these dark hills."

Rick drove into the parking lot and they got out. As the approached the entrance, the door opened and the figure of a woman in a black evening dress appeared, almost as if their approach had been observed, *anticipated*.

She was around fifty, with dyed black hair pulled taught in a bun and she was almost skeletally thin, the tight, black opera gloves looking like her bony hands and forearms had been dipped in ink.

"Well, hello," she said to them. "Welcome to the Mission Hotel."

"Are you the proprietor?" Rick asked.

"I am."

"Miss. Buse?" asked Diane.

The woman frowned. "No, I'm afraid not."

"Rachael Buse?"

The woman shook her head. "My name is Adora Monroy. I'm afraid you've got the wrong person. Can I book you both in for the night? We have some very comfortable rooms."

"Yes, that would be fine," said Rick. "Sorry, we're looking for somebody who is registered at this address. A guest perhaps?"

"Not that I'm aware of," said the hotelier. "But come, I will show you to your rooms. Eduardo with carry your baggage."

"Oh, that's fine," said Diane. "We don't really have any bags. We can get what we need from the camper once we're checked in."

"Very well."

The overdressed lady led them into the lobby and they checked in. The sound of voices, laughter and a soft band came from the dining room. The lady picked up a silver candelabra from the desk and lit their way as they followed her up a wide stairway to the rooms on the upper floor. Rick glanced at Diane, bemused by the rather dramatic need for a candelabra.

"Well, this place doesn't seem too bad," said Rick as they inspected their room after their host had departed. "Clean. Classy. Plenty of other guests, by the sound of it, and we've got the owner herself showing us to our room, eccentric she may be."

"Yes, it's a little too good considering its location," said Diane. "Who are all the other guests? Why are they all staying out here in the middle of nowhere?"

Rick shrugged. "Maybe it's a convention. Now come on, let's freshen up and go down and join them. I need a drink and we're both starved."

They didn't bother changing as it was late and they were ravenous. They were here, that was the important thing, and they could carry on their investigations in the morning when the light of day made a better picture of this strange old hotel.

They found themselves horribly underdressed as they entered the dining room and saw all the couples in their evening wear sitting in small groups at tables around the room. An arched gallery circled the room and the soft candlelight reflected from the gigantic glass chandelier that hung from a mirrored ceiling. The band occupied an alcove on the far side of the room.

Heads turned as they entered, and faces smiled. It was all overly familiar, *weird*. The crowd was a real mixed bunch; some young some very old. Some were couples, others were groups. Nobody sat alone.

A waiter greeted them with the same beaming smile as the other guests and showed them to a table. The other guests had turned their attention back to their meals and to each other, but Rick was aware of several side glances that made him feel deeply uneasy. The band, encouraged by the waiter, started in on another soft lounge number.

The waiter brought them an ice bucket containing a bottle of pink champagne while they perused the menu.

"Oh, we didn't order any champagne," said Rick, his heart set on something a little stronger. He wasn't much of a bubbly drinker.

"Compliments of the house," said the waiter. "Miss Monroy hopes that you will enjoy your stay."

"Well, that's ... very kind of her," said Rick, dismayed that they would have to accept the champagne or appear rude.

The waiter poured out a glass for them each and they ordered their meals; Salisbury Steak for Rick and veal parmesan for Diane.

The couple at the neighboring table were elderly and dressed to the nines. The man glanced over at them as the waiter scurried off.

"Enjoying your stay?"

"Ronald, don't disturb the young couple," said his wife with a frown.

"Oh, that's all right," said Diane. "We just got here as a matter of fact. We feel a little underdressed ..."

"Don't worry about that, my dears," said Ronald. "We're all friends here."

"Really? Do you know everybody here?"

"Oh, yes. We come here every summer. Most of the other guests do too."

"I have to say that we were a little surprised to find so many guests here. This hotel seems like such an out of the way place."

"Well, it wasn't always, you see," said Ronald's wife, apparently happy to contribute to the conversation now. "This used to be a lovely little town. But then they moved the highway and all the businesses moved away. The town shriveled up and died after that."

"But not this place?"

"No, not this place. We like the peace and quiet, you see, and enough of us return year after year to keep the old place in business. It's an ideal retreat. As you said, it's a little out of the way."

"And that's the way we like it," said Ronald. "I'm Dr. Painter, but you can call me Ronald. This is my wife, Marcia."

"I'm Diane. My husband, Rick."

Rick forced a smile and picked up his champagne glass. Chatting to the elderly wasn't at all what he wanted to be doing right now but at least he had some booze to take the edge off. He drank deeply. He was no connoisseur, but it tasted like good stuff. That mad old dame sure knew how to treat new guests.

"Do you stay here all summer?" Diane asked the couple.

"Oh, no. Just a week," Ronald replied. "It's all I can afford to take off. I have my practice to get back to. But a week is more than enough."

"Not much to do around here, I guess," said Rick, feeling like he should at least contribute something to the conversation.

Ronald smiled at him. "Everything we need is right here in the hotel. It offers us perfect relaxation and rejuvenation. But you're right, a week is long enough. After tomorrow, most of us will drift off to our homes."

"Tomorrow?" said Diane. "What happens tomorrow?"

Ronald and his wife shared a glance. Their smiles made Rick think of sharks for some reason. Old, nearly toothless sharks.

"Tomorrow is the solstice, my dear," said Mrs. Painter. "Midsummer. The hotel throws something of a party. You're lucky to be here for that."

Diane's rictus of a smile faded as she looked at Rick. Rick knew what she was thinking. The solstice. A pagan festival. Dancing naked in circles? *The Chorazin Working*? Is that what this gathering of strange coots was all about? Was *this* the cult?

Their meals came and the food was excellent. Rick's newfound taste for champagne saw them finish off the bottle of which Diane only had one glass, and he ordered a whisky. Most of the guests had finished eating now and the band had embarked upon a livelier repertoire. Couples started dancing and everybody seemed to be in high spirits.

"Do you dance?" Ronald asked them.

"Uh, no. Not too much," said Rick. His head was swimming now and he was looking forward to hitting the sack.

"Marcia and I are old romantics," Ronald went on. "It was at a dance that I first captured her heart nearly fifty-two years ago!"

"Fifty-one," his wife corrected him. "And I do believe that it was *I* who asked *you* to dance."

"Quite right, my dear, quite right. Shall we?"

Marica offered her gloved hand and Ronald, slowly rising, took it and led her away from the table. "Do join us!" he said to Rick and Diane over his shoulder. "The more the merrier!"

"I think we'll just head up to our room," said Rick. "It's been a long day."

"Oh, that's a shame," said Marica. "We do like dancing with new couples. Swapping partners for a night does keep a marriage fresh, am I right Ronald?"

Swapping partners? thought Rick. *Christ, are they swingers?* He glanced at Diane. "All finished, Honey?"

Diane nodded and they got up from their seats. Several guests watched them go with the same knowing smiles.

"What the hell is this place?" Rick asked Diane in a hushed voice as they passed through the lobby and made for the stairs.

"I don't know but it's the *right* place, I'm sure of it," she replied.

Rick fetched a few things from the camper and they got ready for bed. The noise drifting up from the dining room kept them awake for a while but their tiredness was too strong to be ignored and soon they fell asleep.

Rick dreamt of the old pump house again.

As always, the Gray Man led him into the darkness by the hand. The circle of robed figures chanted and the dogs barked.

This time, he would look, he promised himself. He would look at the Gray Man's face and find out who he was once and for all. He would unlock the final secret of his dreams and find out who had brought him to that pump house all those years ago.

His whole body trembling with fear, he forced himself to slowly turn his head and look at the ash-gray hand that held his own. His eyes followed it from wrist to elbow and then up to its shoulder and finally saw the head of the Gray Man. It was bald and ashen. And as it turned to look down on him, eyes of fire bored into his.

Rick screamed and awoke drenched in sweat. Diane was still asleep next to him.

Those eyes, he thought. He had seen those eyes before. That same ferocious glare that seemed to strip the skin and flesh from him to peer into the kernel of his soul was familiar to him for he had seen it only yesterday. Those eyes were the same eyes he had seen looking back at him in place of his own reflection in the rearview mirror of the camper when they had set out on their journey to this hotel.

He sat up in bed and cradled his head in his hands. He was going mad, he knew it. Somehow his nightmares were altering his perception of reality and his waking visions were in turn feeding his nightmares so that it was all a feverish mishmash of delusion. What the hell was happening to him and why did it have to happen now that they were so close to their goal? Diane needed him. They were truly in the lion's den now but how could he help her when his own grip on reality was breaking into fragments?

It was then that he realized that the chanting still rung in his ears. It was the same chanting from his dream but it remained in his hearing like tinnitus, distant enough that it had taken him until now to notice it.

A residual effect of his dream? More evidence of his own slipping sanity? Or was it real? The more he focused on it, the more he felt that there really was chanting coming from some deep recess of the hotel.

He got up slowly so as not to wake Diane. His armpit throbbed terribly. The bandage he had wound around it was spotted with blood and extremely tight. The damn thing had gotten bigger! He slowly unwound the wrapping and tossed it in the trash before inspecting the swelling.

It was enormous. A big, angry red bulge that was beaded with sweat. The hole from which he had plucked the hair and the tooth was a puckered sphincter like an asshole. He needed a doctor. This thing would kill him, he was sure of it.

He walked over to the door. Pressing his ear against the wood he could definitely hear the muffled voices of people chanting in unison. Then, a voice whispered in the corridor without. Rick didn't catch the words but his heart hammered in his chest with the knowledge that somebody was right outside their door.

Gently, he unlocked the door and stepped out into the dark corridor. He looked up and down the length of it and caught the brief glimpse of a naked woman peering at him from the gloom, half of her body hidden around the corner.

A soft laugh taunted him as the woman vanished.

What the hell? Rick thought.

He closed the door on his sleeping wife and set off down the corridor, his bare feet noiseless on the soft carpet. He rounded the corridor just in time to see a naked ass and a swish of blonde hair vanish into the darkness.

Knowing that he was being toyed with, Rick's anger grew. As if it wasn't bad enough that they had wound up in this hellish cult convention and that he was gradually turning into Quasimodo, but now these people insisted on playing games with him?

He quickened his pace, keen to give this bitch a piece of his mind. As he rounded the corner he found himself on the gallery that surrounded the dining room. The chanting was louder now and he knew that there were people in the room below him. He could see their shadows cast on the walls by the light of flickering candles.

The naked woman revealed herself by stepping out from one of the alcoves that ran along the gallery. The dim light made deep shadows along the curves of her breasts and the dark patch of hair between her legs. He recognized the face and knew that this game had begun many days ago and ran deeper than he had ever imagined.

She smiled and beckoned a finger.

It was Brenda.

"You!" he said. "My wife was right about you. You're mixed up in this cult, aren't you?"

"We are really nothing you should fear," she said.

"Where is my wife's sister? What have you done with her?"

"This was never about her. She joined us of her own free will. And you want to too, don't you?"

"No!"

She slunk closer to him, like a silky cat, all smooth movements. One hand wandered up to his neck.

"You want me, don't you?"

"No," he said in a quieter, less convincing voice.

"You've wanted me since you first set eyes on me at that camping ground. And I have wanted you."

"Stop it," he said, batting her hand away with his own. The movement caused a shock of pain from the lump in his armpit. He winced and nearly doubled over.

"Oh, my poor Rick," said Brenda. "It hurts doesn't it? But it won't be long now. Why don't you let me take you downstairs and soothe some of that pain."

"How did you ...?"

"I know all about you, Rick. I have for a very long time."

"It was you who painted that symbol on the back of our camper, wasn't it?"

"Yes."

"Why?"

"For your protection. You were never supposed to go to San Diego. That wasn't part of the plan. I tried to persuade you not to go but that wife of yours was so persistent. And after those three teenagers nearly drove you off the road, we have done what we can to keep you from harm."

My God, he thought. *Then it was the cult who murdered those kids.* They had butchered them in order to protect them. But why?

Another jolt of pain from his armpit radiated through his body and he all but collapsed in agony. He could feel it throbbing like it had never done before. Something was going on. Something was writhing about inside of him.

Brenda looped an arm around him and supported his weight. He was very aware of her nakedness pressing against his body. Her mouth was very close to his now and he could feel the heat of her breath on his neck. He tried to think of Diane sleeping in their room a few doors away but found that he couldn't focus on the image. All he could see was Brenda's lips and the thought of kissing them drove all else out of his consciousness.

"Oh, my darling," she said. "Come with me and soon all your pain will be over. Let me introduce you to everybody. They are just dying to meet you properly and you'll find that we really aren't such a bad crowd. To-morrow is an important day of ritual. But tonight, we celebrate."

She helped him down the gallery that overlooked the dining room. There was a party in progress below and as he was afforded a view through the arches, Rick suddenly felt like he was in a world constructed of his nightmares and the horrifying images from the snuff film all rolled into one.

They were naked, young and old, and they were fucking in the light of the candles like snakes in a pit. Limbs glistening with sweat coiled around torsos and fingers dug into tangles of hair. It wasn't all conventional sex either. There were men with men, women with women, some were tied down, contorted into unnatural poses while others cracked whips and abused each other with implements too terrifying for Rick to understand. It was a demonic orgy worthy of the Renaissance painters. All of it was reflected in the ceiling mirror which only served to amplify the disorientating and stomach-churning atmosphere.

One by one, they noticed him and looked up from their debauchery with expressions of ecstatic glee until a sea of wide-eyed faces gazed up at him as if he were an emperor atop a balcony.

"He has come!" they cried. "He has come to us at last!"

Brenda took him by the hand and led him over to the stairs. He followed meekly, feeling like he had lost his mind utterly and existed only in a land of nightmares.

CHAPTER 16

Diane woke late. The morning sun was streaming in through the gap in the curtains and only when the bar of light fell upon her face did she stir from the longest sleep she could remember. She fumbled for her watch on her nightstand and gasped to learn that it was approaching noon. How exhausted had she been last night?

Rick was gone.

His side of the bed was cold so he must have been up and about for hours. How could he go wandering off in this place without waking her first? Seething, she got up and got dressed. Guessing that she had missed breakfast, she headed downstairs in search of Rick.

The hotel was deathly silent. The carousing of last night seemed to have taken its toll on the guests who must all be sleeping off their hangovers now. There was nobody in reception and the dining room was empty.

She did a quick tour of the hotel's ground floor and found no sign of anybody. Then she went outside and found the man Mrs. Monroy had called Eduardo, clipping the bushes at the side of the hotel.

"Have you seen my husband?" she asked him. "Mr. Margold?"

"No, Ma'am," he replied.

"Where is the owner please?"

The man shrugged his shoulders and Diane went back inside in irritation.

She found Mrs. Monroy in reception.

"Ah, good morning Mrs. Margold," she said. "You slept well, I trust?"

"Very, thank you," Diane replied. "Have you seen my husband? He got up before me and I don't know where he's got to."

"No, I'm afraid not. I expect he's taking a walk around the grounds."

"He's not. I've been all over."

"Perhaps he went into town."

"Town? Is there a town? I thought it was deserted."

"Yes, it is rather. Not much to see there, I'm afraid. Is your camper still parked outside?"

"Yes, it is."

"Then your husband can't have gone far."

Realizing that was true, Diane went back up to their room, hoping that Rick had returned from whatever expedition he had been on. But there was still no sign of him. Diane picked up the keys to the Winnebago from Rick's nightstand. It was then that she realized that Rick's pants and shirt still hung over the back of the chair by the window. *His damned clothes are still here.* That meant that he had wandered off in his pajamas.

Starting to get really worried that something was wrong, Diane left the room and went back down to reception. Mrs. Monroy was still there and despite Diane's increasingly frantic tone, she didn't seem to appreciate the strangeness of the situation which only increased Diane's desperation.

"Look, something is wrong, I know it," she insisted. "His clothes are still up in our room. He can't have just vanished in a puff of smoke."

"I really wish I could help you, Mrs. Margold," the hotelier said. "But I haven't the faintest idea where your husband has got to. If you don't mind my asking, did you quarrel last night?"

"Quarrel? No, I ..." She realized that Mrs. Monroy was implying that Rick had stormed off in his pajamas after a fight and presumably hitchhiked to the next town. The idea was so laughable that she refused to entertain it.

She left the reception area and did another tour of the ground floor. Panic grew in her chest like a balloon. After chasing clues all summer trying to find Christine, she just couldn't cope with Rick going missing, not now, not after they had been through so much on this trip. Something bad had happened, she knew it. Just as Christine had vanished, so too had Rick and she knew the same people were responsible.

She noticed a set of double doors that led to another part of the hotel. She tried the handles but found them locked. There was no sign indicating what lay beyond them so she went back to reception.

"Those doors at the end of that corridor," she asked Mrs. Monroy. "Where do they lead?"

"That part of the hotel is closed," said Mrs. Monroy.

"Why?"

"Renovations. We hope to have it open next summer."

"Is it possible that you could show me around back there? In case my husband has somehow wandered in there?"

"Mrs. Margold, there is no way your husband could have wandered in there. It's kept locked at all times."

"But if I could just have a look ..."

"I'm afraid not. There's nothing behind those doors but empty rooms and building supplies. I have been assured that the area is unsafe for guests, hence the locked doors."

Diane knew she was being lied to but was unsure where the lie lay or what the reason behind it was. It was futile to argue with Mrs. Monroy, the woman was an iron-clad wasp. But there had to be someway past her.

Diane went back to the double doors and gazed at them. She looked out of the window and realized that the doors were situated less than halfway along the hotel's eastern wing. There was practically a whole wing of the hotel back there! What was Mrs. Monroy hiding?

She went outside and followed the wall of the hotel's eastern wing. An arched pergola ran along the length of the building and Diane walked in its shade, looking in through the windows. Most of the curtains were drawn but some were open, affording her a view of empty rooms. From the fourth or fifth window onwards, every curtain was drawn. She followed the building around to its other side and saw that all the curtains were drawn on that side too. Whatever renovations were going on in the eastern wing, it seemed that Mrs. Monroy didn't want any prying eyes looking in.

She went back inside and went upstairs. By following the eastern wing to the point that would be directly above the double doors downstairs, she found a blank wall blocking that end of the corridor, papered over.

That made no sense. If a wing of the hotel lay behind that wall, then surely it would be accessible from both floors?

Putting her hands to the wall, she smoothed them over the paper, feeling for any tell-tail signs that a doorway had been covered. The wall was smooth and the paper professionally applied. She rapped the wall with her knuckles, listening for hollowness the way she had seen it done in detective movies. There was definitely a large hollow section in the middle of the wall, right where a pair of doors would be.

Plasterboard, she thought. *Fine. If I can't get in downstairs, then I'll break in upstairs.*

She found a standing lamp fashioned in the figure of a naked man and hefted it in her hands. Not caring if she woke the guests, she swung it at the center of the wall. Its base plunged through plasterboard, leaving a large dent. Wrenching it free, she swung it again.

After a few more swings, she had created a large hole in the wall through which she could see into the hotel's east wing.

It was dark on the other side of that wall and, as she peered through the hole she had made, she could make out a dim corridor, similar to the others in the hotel. But this wing had clearly been disused for a long time. The dust lay thick on the carpet and cobwebs hung from the light fixtures.

She hesitated, expecting Mrs. Monroy or Eduardo or somebody to come running to apprehend her for destroying a wall. But nobody came. The same old silence reigned in the hotel's empty corridors.

The hole was a tight fit and she got a good coating of plaster dust but she was able to squeeze through and found herself on a landing with a stairway that led down to the locked double doors on the ground floor. A corridor stretched away to the farthest end of the building and she crept along, trying a few doors at random. All of them were locked. She returned to the stairs and went down to the ground floor.

Here was some evidence of renovation. Some walls had been knocked through and screens erected. Workmen's tools were stacked up neatly and a linen trolley had been parked at the foot of the stairs.

As she passed it, Diane peered into the trolley's baskets and could see some items of clothing had been tossed in there. They were striped, like men's pajamas.

Like Rick's pajamas.

Diane reached into the linen trolley and pulled out a striped pajama shirt that was flecked with blood. She gasped.

It was Rick's, she was sure of it. Oh, God, what had happened to him? What had they done to him back here in this sealed-off area?

She continued down the corridor, determined to find Rick and get the both of them out of this place alive if possible.

It was dark and the gloom seemed impenetrable. The only light came from some unblocked window deep in the recesses of this abandoned area. Some movement caught her eye and as she peered harder, straining her eyes, she saw the unmistakable shape of a person, rising from the blackness.

The breath caught in her throat as she became paralyzed with terror. Had the figure seen her? Heard her approaching? She couldn't tell if it was a man or a woman for they were silhouetted against the dim daylight. Then, a second figure rose and turned to stare in Diane's direction. Had they been sleeping? What the hell was this place? A third rose and Diane got the impression of a nest of slumbering creatures disturbed by her intrusion.

The figures moved towards her, leaving no doubt in her mind that they had seen her. She turned and ran back the way she had come, back to the stairs. She didn't look back and had no idea if they were following. All she wanted to do was get out of this place, out of this hotel and back on the highway.

But not without Rick.

She reached the hole she had made and squirmed through it, landing face down on the carpet. She was still holding Rick's bloodied pajamas.

Downstairs she found the reception deserted. She dinged on the bell again and again until Mrs. Monroy emerged.

"What the fuck have you done with my husband?" she demanded.

There was no sign of shock on Mrs. Monroy's tight features. "Whatever do you mean, Mrs. Margold?" she said.

Diane held up the bloodied pajamas. "I found these in the sealed off part of the hotel you tried to keep me out of. They are my husband's. They have blood on them."

Mrs. Monroy's cat-like eyes flitted to the bloodied clothing and back to Diane. "I don't know how you got into the east wing but it was most unwise. As for your husband's stained pajamas, I haven't the faintest idea. Perhaps he cut himself and discarded them."

"While wandering around this hotel?" said Diane. "I won't be lied to anymore, Mrs. Monroy. I'm going to call the police. Is there a payphone in the building?"

Mrs. Monroy lifted a black telephone from behind the reception and placed it in front of Diane. "Call the police, by all means," she said. "Perhaps they might be able to find your husband."

Put out a little by the woman's nonchalance, Diane lifted the receiver and dialed 'O'.

"Hello, yes, operator? I'd like the police please."

Mrs. Monroy held Diane's gaze the whole time as she was put through to the local sheriff's department. When the conversation was over, Diane hung up the receiver.

"Well?" Mrs. Monroy asked, eagerly.

"They're sending a deputy," said Diane. "He should be here within half an hour."

"I'm so glad. Perhaps then we can get this whole mess cleaned up."

Diane couldn't take any more of the woman's penetrating eyes or disregard for absolutely everything so she went outside and waited for the deputy. She still clutched the bloodied pajamas. It was all she had left of Rick. All the proof she had that something terrible had happened to him.

It was almost with surprise that she spotted the police car nosing its way up the drive to the hotel, almost exactly half an hour later. So much had gone wrong and their luck had taken such a dive that it wouldn't have surprised her if no cop showed.

She stood up as the car parked and waited for the deputy to get out. He was a middle-aged man with iron-gray hair but a lean, muscular frame that did some good in reassuring Diane that help was here at last.

"Are you the young lady who called the police about a missing fella?" he said.

"Yes, Deputy," Diane replied. "My name's Diane Margold. My husband and I checked in here last night and now he's gone missing. They have a blocked off portion of the hotel back there and I found this." She held out the bloodied pajamas.

The deputy took the garment from her and inspected it.

"They've done something to my husband, Deputy," said Diane as the tears pricked her eyes, threatening to gush. "I just know it." She wasn't going to say anything about the cult or the real reason they were there. She figured the police would find plenty of evidence once they busted this place wide open. She only hoped they wouldn't find Rick's body somewhere inside.

"Just calm yourself, Ma'am," the deputy said. "I'm Deputy Radcliff. Now whatever's happened here, we'll get to the bottom of it. Could be your husband's fine and well and has just gone for a walk or something."

"No, he wouldn't," said Diane. "Not without telling me. He was feeling unwell. He wouldn't have just wandered off."

"Well, first thing's first," said Deputy Radcliff. "I need to speak with the proprietor of this place. Old Adora and I know each other so I'm sure this is all just a misunderstanding."

Diane felt her hopes sinking. This small-town folksy attitude was not what she had wanted from the police.

"It's best if you sit tight while I see what's what,"
Deputy Radcliff continued. "Take a seat in my car. No
telling how long this will take."

Diane followed him over to the car and got in the
back seat. He shut the door and she watched him
through the dust-smeared window as he walked up the
steps to the hotel and disappeared inside.

She sighed and leant back in her seat. Well, it was
up to this cop now. She had done all she could. *Oh,
Rick, where are you?*

The minutes passed and it began to get hot inside
the car. Noticing that it wasn't possible to roll down the
passenger windows, Diane tried to open the door to let
some air in and discovered that the doors were locked.

What the hell? Had Deputy Radcliff accidentally
locked her in? There was no way he would hear her if
she banged on the window so she squirmed her way into
the driver's seat and tried the doors. They were locked
too but at least she was able to roll down one of the windows and get a little air.

Maybe she had been through too much in the past
few days but her suspicions had been aroused and there
was no quietening them. Was this deputy really going to
help her? Or was he going to believe whatever story his
old friend 'Adora' told him? How could she be sure this
guy was even who he said he was? He hadn't even
shown her any identification ...

She reached over and flipped open the glove box.
She just wanted to find some ID that would put her
mind at rest. The compartment was filled with junk but
she spotted a laminated card lurking at the back. She
dug it out and saw that it belonged to Deputy Jack Radcliff. A sob welled up inside her when she saw that the
picture of the tubby, bespectacled Deputy Radcliff bore
no resemblance to the man she had just spoken to.

It was all so hopeless. He was one of them, truly an 'old friend' of Mrs. Monroy. She couldn't even call the police. The switchboard girl she had spoken to was in on it too. They probably had her stashed in some room in the hotel. It was all rigged. She had to get out of there.

She tried the door and, remembering that it was locked, began squirming her way out through the driver's window.

"Hey!" came a cry as she slithered down onto the dusty ground beside the cop car.

She looked up and saw the false Deputy Radcliff hurrying down the steps towards her.

Shit!

She was on her feet and running before her pursuer had covered even half the distance to the car. Slipping and sliding, she made her way down the steep incline that sloped away from the hotel towards the town.

She heard the car engine start up and didn't look back as she half stumbled, half ran through a patch of pine trees. She emerged on the road that led through the abandoned town. The cop car was making its way down the drive from the hotel, and she knew she would be spotted if she hung about. A row of boarded up buildings faced her on the other side of the road and she ran for them, slipping down an alley overgrown with weeds just as the cop car came around the bend and passed down the street.

CHAPTER 17

When Rick awoke, he found himself in what looked like a hotel room and for a brief moment, he believed that Brenda and the orgy was just some bizarre fever dream. But when he sat up and realized that he was wearing some sort of hospital gown and that the room he was in bore little resemblance to the one he had gone to bed with Diane in, his terror returned.

There was no furniture other than the bed and a small side table with a glass of water on it. He reached for the water and then, hesitantly withdrew his hand. He trusted nothing in this hellish hotel.

The orgy had been real. He remembered Brenda leading him down the stairs to the dining room where naked people fawned over him and pawed at his body, revolting him with their lecherous grasps. He had clung to Brenda as if seeking her protection from her vile cultist friends. She had acquiesced and had guided him through the throng, guarding him as if he belonged to her. They had sat down on a red leather sofa and he remembered her giving him something to drink. She had kissed him and stroked his face as the pain in his armpit had subsided.

He remembered nothing after that.

He had no idea how long he had been out. Where were his pajamas? Why was he dressed like some sort of mental patient? And what had happened to Diane? He got up and went to the door to try the handle. Locked, predictably. So, he was a prisoner of this crazy cult. Is this what had happened to Christine? Is this what they had done to that girl in the snuff film? Was that to be his fate? So many questions ...

The pain in his armpit returned and he only just made it back to the bed without collapsing on the floor in agony. It had got so bad! He curled up in a ball on the bed and screamed out his pain and fear in one long, animalistic howl.

After a time, the door opened. He hadn't the strength to make a run for it, to push past his captors and run through the hotel screaming Diane's name. A dark, spider-like figure entered the room. It was Mrs. Monroy.

"How are you feeling, my dear?" she asked.

"What are you doing to me?" he demanded.

"We're doing nothing," she said. "Merely looking after you."

"Looking after me? I've been drugged, stripped naked and locked up in this madhouse! Where is my wife?"

"Your wife is safe."

"Stop with your lies!" Rick screamed. "I know what you are! I know what you've been doing and now you want to silence us! You've been watching us this whole time, haven't you? Following us as we looked for my wife's sister."

"Yes, we have been watching," she replied. "But you mistake our intentions. We have been watching over you, trying to protect you. You in particular, Rick."

"Protect me from what?"

"All manner of things. It was of the utmost importance that you came to us unharmed and at the right time. That is why we took measures."

"Brenda."

"Yes. She did well but not as well as you, my dear. You have done much of our work for us. We did not foresee how well you would protect yourself."

"I don't understand."

"Those three youths for instance. They very nearly upset everything."

"The teenagers who tried to run us off the road? You had them killed. But why try to frame me?"

She chuckled. "*We* did not kill them. *You* did."

"Me?" Rick was outraged. The idea was so absurd. He thought back to the gruesome scene in the back of the van. The dead teenagers. The bloodied axe embedded in one of their skulls. The axe in his hand. Him swinging it ...

Wait.

Other images superimposed themselves on his perception of the past. Images of the woods as he left the camper. Memories of his sleep being disturbed by some noise. He saw the side locker, broken into. He heard tittering laughter and saw three figures running off through the darkness towards the road. He saw his own hands grasp the axe from inside the locker. He saw the van with the wizard painted on the side. He saw his own hands fling open the back doors, the terrified faces of the kids inside, the spattering of blood as he swung the axe into the face of the tall boy ...

"Oh, God!" he moaned.

"Such savagery!" Mrs. Monroy crooned. "Such an impressive primal will to survive! And then that interfering police man too ..."

"Garrett?" Rick asked. "What about him? I didn't do anything to him ..."

"On the contrary," said Mrs. Monroy. "You pushed him from an upper story window. He survived, but you bought yourself enough time to get away. Well done, my dear."

An unbidden memory from that night in the abandoned farmhouse returned to Rick. He had seen Garrett's flashlight illuminating the walls of the stairwell as he climbed, heard his voice identifying himself. Rick had hidden in one of the bedrooms, waited until Garrett was on the landing and then ... he had run at him, pushing him back towards the window.

Jesus Christ! He had truly gone insane, hadn't he? What else lay in the murkiness of his subconscious? How many other people had he murdered?

Then he remembered the mugger that night in Queens when he had been in his early twenties. He had been on his way home from his first date with Diane. The guy had pulled a knife and demanded his wallet. Rick had hit him, knocked him down, picked up the guy's knife and then ...

"Why?" he moaned. "Why didn't I remember any of this?"

"Because your mind blocked it out," said Mrs. Monroy. "It truly is a marvelous organ. It has been protecting you all this time, even from yourself. You are special, Rick. you have carried something with you nearly your entire life. Something deep within you that rises to the surface to protect you when danger threatens. You were gifted with this when you were six years old."

"The pumphouse," said Rick. "That was you people, wasn't it?"

"Well, yes and no. There are many such groups as ours across the United States, across the world even. The names and organizational structure of these groups has always been a fluid thing but our common goal is always constant."

"And that is?"

"Our utter devotion to the worship of Satan."

"You people are insane ..."

"No. The world is insane and it needs a cleanse. Centuries of false prophets and corrupt religions based on guilt and slavery have brought it to the brink of annihilation. War and persecution and dogma and brutality have kept humanity bogged down since we emerged from the cradle of civilization. It is time for the true lord to rise once more and usher in a new age, an age of primal purity! An age of simplicity where only the flesh is hallowed and all gods die by the hands of those who fashioned them!"

It was all so crazy that Rick could have laughed in the mad woman's face. But his experiences of the past few weeks robbed the situation of any humor. He had seen things, done things that somehow made him complicit in all of this. He didn't understand how but he felt that he had always been a part of it, ever since that night beneath Untermeyer Park in 1953. That was where it had begun.

"Who was the gray man who brought me to the pumphouse?" he asked.

"Gray man?"

"Was it the devil?"

Mrs. Monroy frowned. "My poor man. Nobody brought you to the pump house. You came of your own free will."

"I ... No ... That's not true! I remember ... I remember him! I've seen his eyes in my dreams!"

"*He* was clearly a figment of your imagination. It was a lot for a child to go through, we appreciate that, but your young mind must have conjured an explanation for why and how you came to us. So you created this demonic figure to cover the truth, just as you blotted out the memories of your magnificent murders, to protect your mind which has been coddled and dulled by the superstitions and selective judgements of your Christian society."

Another jolt of pain rocked Rick's body to the core and the swollen flesh of his armpit felt like it was about to burst.

"Doctor!" Mrs. Monroy said and Dr. Painter from dinner last night hustled into the room, his medical case in hand.

Squatting by the bed, Dr. Painter tenderly touched Rick's armpit over the material of his hospital gown. The slightest pressure sent Rick into spasms of pain.

"My poor man," said the doctor. "How you suffer for Our Lord. We must remove this gown so that I may have a better look."

Despite his pain, Rick wasn't about to let this mad satanist probe him even if he was a doctor but his resistance proved futile for two other men squeezed into the room and manhandled him out of his gown.

Lying naked on the bed in front of an audience, Rick wished that he could just die. This desire only increased when he looked down at his throbbing armpit and saw that the swelling had increased to the size of a football, the puckered opening quivering, kissing the thin air. The inflamed skin was stretched taught and the whole thing looked like it might rupture at any moment.

"The time has almost come!" said Dr. Painter. "We must hurry to make our preparations!"

"It is all well in hand, my good doctor," said Mrs. Monroy.

Rick writhed as more pain blossomed from the swelling to flood his being. Between his agonized spasms, He got the distinctive feeling of movement in his armpit and for the first time, the horrifying thought struck him.

Dear God, is there something living in there?

The sun had begun to set over the hills making the shadows between the abandoned buildings deeper. Diane had spent the past couple of hours hiding in a building with broken windows and no doors. She figured it had once been a store but now it was an empty shell that provided her with some sort of cover from her pursuer.

She had heard the cop car slowly rolling down the streets of the ghost town, its driver no doubt peering down every alleyway for a sign of her. As far as she could tell, he hadn't gotten out of the car for which she was thankful. If he started poking through these ruins on foot, she had no doubt that he would find her eventually. As it was, she was able to sneak into places a car couldn't follow.

It had been at least an hour since she had heard the crunch of its tires and she dared to hope that he had moved on, either back to the hotel or to wherever his nearby haunt was. With darkness approaching, she had no desire to remain in these ruins in the company of their ghosts.

She knew now that her only hope of survival was to get the hell out of there and back to civilization. Rick might be alive or he might be dead but there was nothing she could do about it now. There was no help to be had here, no way of calling the police.

And no vehicle to escape in either.

That was the thing that really worried her. There wasn't a single abandoned car in this ghost town and, as she and Rick had noted last night, there didn't seem to be any cars up at the hotel either. No doubt they had all been hidden away somewhere to prevent their escape. That just left the Winnebago.

She still had the keys. If she could get back up to the hotel unnoticed, she had a chance of escaping. They would hear her start the engine and would no doubt give pursuit, but with no vehicles of their own, she should be able to make a fast getaway.

The thought of going back up that hill to the hotel filled her with dread. But there was no other way around it. If she wanted to get out, if she wanted help Rick, then she had to try.

Poking her head out the broken doorframe, she made sure there was no sign of the cop car. It wasn't far to the main road that ran along the foot of the hill upon which the hotel stood. Keeping as quiet as possible, she stole through the town towards the road.

The deepening shadows seemed to clutch at her as she ran. Up ahead, she could see the hotel looming against the reddening sky, its mission bell and stringy palms black silhouettes. She crossed the road and made her way back up through the pines, the same way she had come down, keeping clear of the snaking curve of the drive.

Some lights were on in the hotel – evidence that its guests were up and about – but there was a larger source of light to the side of the building. As she emerged from the trees, she could hear and smell burning as of some roaring bonfire. Some satanic ritual? Images of witches capering around a fire were conjured in Diane's head and she tried to dismiss them. All she had to do now was get to the Winnebago without being seen and then she was away!

She kept her head low as she hurried over to the pergola. Then, making her way through the bushes, she rounded the building to the parking lot at the rear.

Then, she saw the cause of the fire.

She rose, her hand to her mouth, tears of desperation stinging her eyes as much as the smoke and acrid stench of burning rubber and plastic did. The shape of the Winnebago was visible within the roaring inferno. Its interior had already been gutted by the flames which pushed their way out through the broken windows. A couple of the tires had already blown, making the burning vehicle lean to one side.

It was gone. Their home from home, their big investment, *their baby*, was gone. And so too was her means of escape.

She could do nothing but stand and stare at the ruin of her chances, the ruin of everything as the smoke billowed up into the evening air. She was done. No other opportunities presented themselves in her mind. *They* had won.

She was aware of figures moving towards her on her left. Startled, she turned to face them, and her mouth fell open in horror.

They were everywhere. They stood on the pergola, even in the upstairs windows of the hotel. She recognized them. Dr. Painter and his wife from last night were there. Brenda was there. *Frank the librarian* was there too and she realized that she had been played with from the very beginning. Everybody she had met since arriving in California had lied to her. They all looked at her with the same expression of patronizing pity.

"You've returned to us, my dear," said Mrs. Monroy as she approached to put her arm on her shoulder.

Diane didn't shrink from her touch. What would be the point? The finality of it all stripped away her instinct to resist.

"Come," said Mrs. Monroy. "The games are over. The time is approaching and we want you to be part of it. Your husband is waiting."

"Rick's ... alive?"

"Oh, yes. We have been taking good care of him. He is in dreadful pain, you understand, but soon it will be over. Soon it will be *done*."

Feeling delirious, as if she were walking through a nightmare, Diane let Mrs. Monroy lead her away from the blazing camper and towards the steps of the hotel.

Chapter 18

There was a sense of great excitement within the hotel, as if something of great import was going to happen shortly. Everybody was dressed in their best like they had been the night before and champagne was being served. Diane refused a glass, disturbed by the ludicrousness of her captors offering her champagne.

Mrs. Monroy took her to a room on the top floor of the hotel and Diane found herself admitted to a luxurious suite with pink carpets, glass chandeliers and expensive-looking furniture. Sideboards and tables were cluttered with silver framed photographs of various people and gatherings, most of which, Diane assumed, were the cult in its earlier days. In fact, she spotted a photograph of Alistair McCreedy in a position of some honor on the mantle above the room's rose-painted fireplace.

"You recognize my father, no doubt," said Mrs. Monroy, following Diane's gaze.

Diane blinked and looked from the photograph to the woman beside her, remembering the sad twelve-year-old girl with the black pigtails in the family portrait. "*You* are Persephone McCreedy?"

"I was once," Mrs. Monroy sighed. "I have gone by many names. Being the daughter of an avowed occultist does make it difficult for one to keep a low profile."

"So you followed your father's work, even after you were fostered at the age of twelve?"

"They tried to keep it from me and partially succeeded for I mostly forgot about my previous life. But I learned the truth when I reached adulthood and then there was nothing they could do to keep me from my heritage."

"Heritage?"

"My father's work. He was on the verge of greatness, you understand. But nearly all was destroyed by those local clods whose minds were too tiny to comprehend his genius. Fortunately some of his followers remained, driven underground by all the bad press of course. They sought me out and welcomed me with open arms as my father's successor. Only after I had studied under their tutelage, and had learned everything my father had discovered, only *then* were we able to try and bring his work to fruition."

"The Chorazin Working," said Diane. "The birth of the antichrist. You people are mad, and so was your father!"

"Mad is a word used by those who do not believe, and they do not believe because they have not *seen*. Soon you will eat your words, my dear, and then perhaps you will be willing to join our ranks."

"Join you! You must be joking."

Mrs. Monroy – Persephone McCreedy – smirked at this. "Your reluctance is anticipated. I would not believe either, were I in your shoes. But you have not seen the things I have seen, or worked the magick I have worked. I too have approached the verge of despair and skepticism on occasion. The Chorazin Working is no easy task. In fact, it has never been achieved, not even by my father. He was so close. All those missing children, poor babies! But individual life is irrelevant in the quest of what can be achieved! My early attempts at my father's rituals threw me into doubt too, made me question my father's work."

"Your early attempts ..." said Diane. "Like that boy in Newport Beach. You were the nanny ... Rachael Buse."

"Ah, yes. You have done your research, my dear. Yes, I was a deal younger then and more arrogant. I hadn't perfected the first part of the ritual."

"First part?"

She smiled. "For the Chorazin working to be effective, the groundwork must be laid first. The *seed* must be planted. Several decades earlier, in fact. Our New York sect facilitated the ritual, and we were finally able to achieve the first part. I have spent the last few years collecting everything my father wrote, preparing myself so that nothing will go wrong with the final part of the ritual."

"Your father's book from the El Toro library," said Diane.

"Yes, I have spent some considerable time hunting down every last copy of my father's work, partly to stop it falling into the wrong hands. He wanted to leave his mark on the world, you see. Vanity was perhaps his only failing. But I couldn't have his rituals floating around for any Tom, Dick or Harry to use. That magick is too dangerous, too valuable."

"I've heard about all the bullshit I'm able to," said Diane. "I don't care about your crazy rituals or your lunatic father's work. I just want to know what you've done with my husband and my sister!"

"Very well," said Mrs. Monroy with a sigh. "I shall be frank then. Your sister, I'm afraid, was a ruse."

Diane stared at the woman, not comprehending her. "A ruse?"

"To bring you here. We are a far-reaching network of believers and we were able to use our New York sect to lure your sister to California knowing full well that you would follow in her footsteps. I have to say, young Christine played her part beautifully. Then it was just a matter of leaving some little clues to help you on your way. We were caused some considerable worry by your unexpected jaunt to San Diego but I am to understand that was due to some evidence we were unable to scrub from the motel room of Detective Ed Milton."

"You killed him, didn't you?"

"We cannot afford loose ends."

"And my sister? Is she ...?"

"I'm afraid so. She outlived her usefulness."

Diane choked back a sob, refusing to cry in front of this woman. Her legs felt weak and she desperately wanted to sit down but remained strong in the face of her tormentor.

"If you knew the true number of lives taken in our efforts, you may see things in a greater perspective."

"You people have murdered your way through the past forty years. All to bring me here? Why? Why me? You keep talking about birthing the antichrist so I guess it's some scheme to impregnate me with the seed of Satan, is that it? Somebody watched *Rosemary's Baby* one too many times?" She laughed despite herself. "I hate to break it to you, sister, but there's a slight hitch in your plans. I can't have babies. I'm sterile. So nothing you psychos do to me will result in me giving birth to the antichrist."

"You?" Mrs. Monroy said with an amused smile. "I was speaking in the plural. Goodness, my dear. Why ever did you think that it was *you* we wanted?"

There was a knock at the door.

"Come!" said Mrs. Monroy.

Frank entered. He gave Diane a small smile, almost apologetic. Diane gave him a scathing look. "The time approaches, High Priestess," Frank said. "The host is in some considerable pain. We have made the preparations."

"Good." Mrs. Monroy looked to Diane. "Come with me, my dear. All will be made clear to you in just a few moments. Decades of work is about to come to fruition."

Diane found herself following them out and back downstairs where the party in the lobby appeared to be in full swing.

"Brothers and sisters!" Mrs. Monroy said, clapping her hands and raising them high. "The hour is upon us!"

She went over to the double doors leading to the sealed off part of the hotel and, drawing a key from a chain around her neck, unlocked them. Frank and another cultist swung them wide and there was a surge of bodies as everybody pressed forward, eager to pass through the doors.

Mrs. Monroy stood to one side, smiling at her underlings as they filed past her. When the last stragglers had gone in, she walked over to Diane and led her by the hand. Frank and the other cultist closed the doors behind them.

The corridor which Diane had ventured down that morning led to some sort of auditorium. A horseshoe of tiered benches took up the end of the wing, spanning both floors and she smelled fresh sawdust. The focal point of the auditorium was something hidden behind hospital screens. The whole place had the feel of a nineteenth-century operating room, though what sort of operation they were about to witness, she couldn't guess.

The auditorium had been constructed to accommodate the whole cult but only just as they had to stand shoulder to shoulder. Mrs. Monroy and Diane stood to one side of the stage.

"Dr. Painter?" Mrs. Monroy called. "Are you ready?"

The elderly doctor emerged from behind the screen dressed in a surgeon's scrubs. "Yes, High Priestess," he said. "The subject is conscious but anesthetized."

"Very good." She turned to Diane. "Dr. Painter is an accomplished surgeon. We're lucky to have him. He's one of the best in his field."

"Even if he is as mad as the rest of you," said Diane bitterly.

"You'd be surprised how many different walks of life exist in our ranks."

"I must say, you put on a surprising show of rational thought for a group of bat-crazy satanists."

"What were you expecting? Robes and candles? Worm-eaten tomes on black altars? Darling, that's just for the tourists. All that drama looks good on film for the perverts but it really serves no purpose."

"Then it is you people who make those snuff films?"

"One of our subsidiary sects. Eager youngsters for the most part. They don't see much in our movement beyond the sex and the drugs but they have their uses. Those films really are most profitable. After my father's demise, we ran embarrassingly short of funds and had to get creative. Fortunately, there is a public fascination with satanism even if few understand it in any detail."

Diane shivered. The way this woman casually talked about murder chilled her to her core.

Cultists came and removed the hospital screens. There was an intake of breath from the crowd in appreciation. When Diane saw who was on the operating table an involuntary scream forced its way through her lips.

Rick lay naked before them, his arms strapped to wings on the table making him appear Christ-like. There was something red in his armpit and the closer Diane looked, the more it looked like an enormous abscess.

"What have you done to him?" she shrieked. "What have you done to my husband?"

"Your husband is the key to a new eon!" Mrs. Monroy said. "He has carried and nurtured the seed for nigh on twenty-five years! Now it is time for the antichrist to hatch and ascend!"

"What is that thing?" said Diane, her eyes focused on the hideous bulge that, whether due to a trick of the light or her own tired and distraught state, seemed to undulate as if there were something moving inside it.

"That is the result of decades of work," Mrs. Monroy replied. "And Mr. Margold has been such a good mother to it. His pain has almost driven him to madness but he kept his sanity. He defended his child through his long journey to us."

"No!" said Diane. "That's not possible! He didn't have that ... that ... *thing* under his arm until now."

"My dear, he has had it since he was six years old. It was a small thing to begin with, just a seed, but it grew. It grows still. It has outgrown your husband, as you can see and is now ready for the next stage in its development. Its pupal stage is over and now, with the help of Dr. Painter, it will begin its imago."

Dr. Painter, assisted by two cultists also dressed in surgical scrubs, picked up a scalpel from a stainless-steel trolley. As he turned his attention to Rick, Diane called out.

"Rick! Rick it's me! Rick!"

Rick's head moved but he did not try to sit up. He could clearly hear her, but he was heavily drugged."

As Dr. Painter's scalpel pressed against the bulging mass beneath Rick's armpit, Diane tried to fight her way to the stage. Mrs. Monroy had been ready for this and, at a nod from her, two cultists rushed forward to restrain her.

"Rick! No!" she wept, struggling between the arms of her captors.

The scalpel cut through the growth and a gush of blood and clear fluid seeped out to run off the table and spatter on the polished wooden floor of the stage. Rick twisted in his bonds a little and a faint groan escaped his lips.

"He can feel it!" Diane cried. "He can feel it, you fools, don't you see? You're hurting him!"

"Hardly," said Dr. Painter through his surgical mask. "He may feel some discomfort but I can assure you that I anesthetized him sufficiently to keep him free form any actual pain."

The doctor continued cutting into the growth until some movement within caused him to drop his scalpel in surprise. "It's here!" he shrieked from the stage. "It has arrived!"

The assembled cult gasped in ecstasy, every one of them leaning forward over the barriers to catch a glimpse of what lay within Rick's mutilated armpit.

Diane was afforded the closest view of the stage and what she saw wriggling and pushing its way out of the incision Dr. Painter had made in her husband, made her feel like the last vestiges of her sanity were fleeing her mind.

It couldn't be true, could it? What hideous, parasitic thing of that size could have grown in Rick's body in such a short time? It had to be a trick, some special effect they were utilizing like in Hollywood movies. This just couldn't be real ...

And then the thing screamed.

It was almost a baby's scream or a blasphemous parody of one. It echoed around the chamber and the assembly cooed in rapturous praise. Dr. Painter, his hands shaking terribly for a surgeon, reached down and pulled the thing loose.

It was a worm of some sort, fat and stubby like a pale grub with the merest indication of two arms and two legs studding its ringed body. Its head was the most hideous thing about it for even at a distance, Diane could see that it had the face of a human newborn.

Dr. Painter held it up for all to see and they erupted in thunderous applause.

"Look upon the antichrist!" Mrs. Monroy cried. "The Son of Satan! Born of man, born to destroy God!"

"Hail Satan!" the crowd shouted. "Hail the Son of Man!"

Diane watched the twitching body of her husband, now forgotten by the crowd. Blood still seeped from his armpit where the folds of flesh hung limp like a deflated balloon.

"My husband, he's bleeding out!" she cried but her voice was lost amid the uproarious celebration. "Somebody please see to my husband!" she screamed.

"Hail Satan!" came the reply. "Hail the antichrist!"

"Please! Somebody!"

She tried to make her way down to the stage but was held back by half a dozen cultists, their gleeful faces and blasphemous cries clouding her senses. She fought and struggled but it was useless. The ghastly thing that had been pulled from Rick's body was all that mattered in the world to them.

CHAPTER 19

Perhaps a day had passed. Perhaps a year. There was no way of telling in this room. There weren't even any clocks. Diane knew only that she was being kept here in this hotel, against her will. And that Rick was dead.

Nobody came to help him. They had left him there on the operating table like a piece of meat, discarded, his worth to them run out.

Damn those bastards to Hell where they belonged!

Every so often she heard *It* screaming. So like a human child but she knew that it was anything but.

They brought her food and decent food too. It was always Frank who knocked on her door, three times a day, bearing her meals on a silver tray. She guessed he had been given this job due to the trust they had once shared. All she wanted to do was throw the food in his face and stab him to death with the cutlery.

But she kept her cool. If she had any hope of escaping this place, then she had to play along, act docile and not let them see her as a threat. They were keeping her alive for a reason. That reason was, as far as she could guess, to make her an eventual member of their sick cult. She knew too much about their operations so there was no way they would let her go free and she knew they were not above murdering anybody they found inconvenient. They wanted to convert her, she was sure of it. All she had to do was show slow but steady compliance – but not rush it, else they suspect some trickery – until the time was right for her to make her move.

There was a bell pull in her room and a visible lead that ran along the ceiling to a point where it vanished into a hole. She tested it one time and heard a distant ringing. Frank soon came hurrying in.

"What's wrong?" he demanded.

"Nothing, I just wanted to see what this bell pull did," Diane replied.

"It calls me, is what it does, Diane," said Frank. "Emergencies only so please don't misuse it."

And with that knowledge, Diane began to formulate her plan.

She waited a few days and did her best to show that she was adjusting to her captivity, even striking up friendly conversation with Frank a few times, as if they were back in the library in El Toro. Privately she wondered what had happened to the previous librarian before Frank was planted in their job. Were they another unwitting casualty in the cult's ruthless plans?

She chose the nighttime to make her move when the hotel was silent. The previous day she had asked Frank for more pillows, claiming that she was uncomfortable. She used these to stuff under her blanket, plumping and shaping them to make it appear that there was a person in the bed. It was a classic trick kids used to fool their parents when they snuck out but, in the dim moonlight streaming in through the windows, the effect was quite convincing.

She steeled herself for what she was about to do. Once she tugged on that bellpull, there would be no going back. Seizing the heavy glass ash tray from her nightstand, she emptied the ash out onto the carpet and gave the bellpull a good yank.

Frank took his sweet time in coming, indicating that he had been fast asleep. That was good. She hoped the whole damn cult was slumbering in their beds. They had to be for this to work.

Diane kept herself concealed in the deep shadow cast by the wardrobe and watched Frank come into the room. He walked straight up to the bed, asking Diane what was wrong. By the time Diane had crept up behind him, he had extended a finger and was prodding the mass of pillows beneath the blanket. Maybe he figured the ruse, maybe not. It didn't matter. Diane slugged him with the glass ashtray and he went down with a grunt.

Exiting her room, she made for the lobby, the soft carpet of the stairs absorbing any noise she made. Passing through the dining room, she made for the kitchen in search of a weapon with which to defend herself.

It was so dark in the kitchen that she had trouble finding her way about. She didn't want to turn on the lights for fear of alerting Eduardo or whoever else might be roaming the hotel, so she made her way slowly, guided only by feel and the dim moonlight that streamed in through the high windows. She found a knife block and selected a good-sized carving knife. It felt good in her hand and with its comforting weight, her confidence in her plan increased as she went back out into the lobby.

Behind the desk she found the keys to the front door. Hurrying across the lobby, she locked the doors and then made her way to the bar area.

Bottles of booze glistened on their racks. She grabbed one of the curtains and yanked it down from its hanging with a ripping sound. Bundling it up, she stuffed it into an ashtray stand. Then, she went behind the bar and selected a bottle of bourbon. Unscrewing it, she emptied about half of it into the ashtray stand. The other half she used to splash over the other curtains. She fetched another couple of bottles from the bar, the highest proof she could make out in the dim light and began emptying them over the velvet upholstered chairs and carpets, making trails towards the curtains.

Then, she grabbed a matchbook from the jar on the bar and twisted one off. Striking it, she touched it to the other matches in the book and watched as they all caught in a brilliant white flame. Taking a deep breath, she tossed the blazing matchbook into the ashtray stand and stood back.

It took a little longer than she had predicted but eventually, the alcohol-soaked curtain caught and within seconds the top of the ashtray stand was a blazing ball of fire. Stooping, so as to keep her face as far from the flames as she could, she picked up the ashtray stand by its stem and moved it towards the curtains. They caught immediately and she barely had time to get out of reach before the curtains became sheets of flames that licked at the ceiling.

It was done. There was no turning back now. This hotel would burn to the ground with every cult member asleep in their rooms. She *could* escape now. She *should*, perhaps, but there was one thing she wanted to be sure of before she left. She wanted to be sure that the abomination that had been birthed from Rick's armpit was dead. She couldn't go through life wondering if that *thing* still lived. She squeezed the handle of her kitchen knife in determination. She had to take care of it herself.

The doors to the east wing were open and she passed down the dim corridor towards the makeshift operating theater at the far end. There was a light up ahead, and she crept towards it; a sliver of warm light showing through the gap between black velvet drapes that screened the operating theater. Creeping up to the drapes, Diane peeped through.

Candles ringed the stage upon which Rick had been killed. The floor had been cleaned of his blood and the operating table had been replaced with a baby's cot, done up in black lace and velvet. The way the cot stood center stage, ringed by the tiered audience stand, made it obscenely reminiscent of an idol in a temple.

Diane pushed her way through the curtains and approached the stage. She could see something within the cot move beneath a black blanket. Her stomach knotted with revulsion, she stepped up onto the stage, the knife poised in her hand.

There was a sound to her right and a figure lurched from some recess in the shadows and flung itself at Diane. The person was naked and blonde hair flailed around an enraged face. Diane just had time to recognize Brenda before she was upon her, knocking her to the wooden floor of the stage.

The knife clattered from her grasp. She raised her hands to protect herself from the flurry of blows Brenda rained down on her face and chest as the crazed woman straddled her and tried to beat her to death.

With a twist of her hips and a shove, Diane sent the lighter woman sprawling to one side and scrambled to get away from her. Brenda rolled onto all fours and looked for a moment like a snarling beast. Diane seized the knife just as Brenda pounced. She slashed the blade at her attacker and caught Brenda across the face. Blood immediately ran from the wound and spattered the stage. Brenda briefly registered that she had been hurt. Her hand went up to her ruined face and touched the nose that was almost severed. But her obsessive duty to protect the thing in the cot superseded her concern for her own welfare and she charged at Diane again.

This time Diane held the knife outwards, point first. Brenda impaled herself on the knife, her mouth sucking in a lungful of air as she realized her mistake. Her fists still beat at Diane, machinelike in their relentlessness. Diane screamed in horror at the situation and in horror of what she had been made to do as she ripped the knife from Brenda's belly and then sunk it in again, this time higher, somewhere below the heart.

Brenda sank to her knees. Blood pumped from her body and swept across the floorboards. Tears of rage and terror streaked Diane's face. She ripped the blade free and watched Brenda die at her feet, cradling her leaking torso.

When she was sure that the thing's guardian was dead, Diane approached the cot once more. She could smell smoke seeping through the corridor as the western end of the hotel burned. It might have been her imagination but she thought she could hear screams too.

The thing in the cot gurgled and sounded so like a baby that Diane was briefly deterred from her mission. For so long she had wanted to hear that sound, the sound of her own baby. But God had denied her that. Worse, he had twisted everything around so that she must be forced to listen to a baby's gurgle while she plunged a knife into it. It wasn't fair. Who was God to use her like this?

She peered over the edge of the cot and looked down at the thing within. *Rick's baby*. The baby she had been unable to give him. The baby they had wanted and had been denied.

Its face had matured much in so short a time. No longer the squashed, purplish visage of a newborn, the alert eyes of a baby looked about, wide awake and eager to drink in all it saw. Its cheeks were chubby and its small mouth spoke soundless words.

Diane reached in and pulled off the black blanket that covered it.

It had changed. No longer a maggot, it's stubby arms and legs had grown into proper limbs. Its body, still round and ridged was morphing into the proper proportions of a human infant. This thing was adapting. It would continue to grow, continue to adapt, camouflaging itself, embedding itself into human society, waiting until the time was right. It *must* be killed.

Her heart feeling like it was being torn from her chest, Diane raised the knife over the baby. It registered

the movement and it looked up at the poised blade. It
spluttered a questioning gurgle.

Diane looked into the eyes of the antichrist. And
the antichrist looked right back into hers and saw deep
into her soul and knew that she wasn't going to do it.

EPILOGUE

Detective Garrett gazed at the smoldering wreckage of the hotel. The fire crews were still dousing water on parts of it which gave off great gushes of steam. One wing had utterly collapsed while the other still stood, or at least, what was left of it. Its white plaster was charred black by the flames that had been forced through every window and most of the roof was gone.

Not being in Orange County, this hotel fire was out of Garrett's jurisdiction but he had made sure the sheriffs in the surrounding counties had also been notified to look out for a 1976 Winnebago Chieftain with a New York plate. They appeared to have found it, or at least its blackened shell parked around the back of the building.

"Doesn't seem close enough to the hotel to have caught fire," said Garrett.

"A stray spark may have ignited it," said Sheriff Cole. "Although those pines over there somehow survived. Personally I'm amazed we don't have a forest fire on our hands." He handed a charred license plate to Garrett. It was twisted and scorched but the letters and numbers were still legible. "This the one you were looking for?"

"Yes," said Garrett. "That's them. What the hell happened here?"

"That's what we're trying to figure out. They're still pulling bodies out. We count twenty-two so far. Place must have been doing good business for being so out of the way like this."

"Then how come the camper is the only vehicle in the lot?" Garrett asked. "Where are all the others?"

"There's a funny thing about that," said Sheriff Cole. "We found a stash of parked cars down in the town."

"Stash?"

"I say stash because it looks like somebody hid them away from view. They're jammed door to door in an abandoned factory. They haven't been there that long either and their license plates are from all over America. Mighty odd for a place nobody passes through anymore."

"You figure they belong to the recently deceased guests?"

"Seems so. But like I said, it's strange as hell. And why is this camper not with them? Why is it parked here? What do you know about these people, Detective?"

"Well, one or two things that don't seem to add up without any context. What can you tell me about this place?"

The sheriff shrugged. "Not a lot to tell. Used to be a popular place before they moved the highway. To be honest, I'm surprised it's still standing. I haven't been through here in a while. The town down there is a ghost town and most of us just figured that the hotel would have gone the same way. But one of my boys has been looking into it this morning and he found out that somebody bought the place about ten years ago; a Mrs. Adora Monroy. Nobody knows much about her but there's talk in the next town about wild parties being held here and convoys of vehicles coming down this way every once in a while. Seems to have been some sort of secret club, at least that's how people figure it and I'm inclined to agree with them. Now, how about this couple of yours?"

"Richard and Diane Margold," said Garrett. "I don't quite know what to make of them. New Yorkers. They claimed to be in California looking for the wife's sister and think that she got wound up in some sort of cult. But there's more they weren't telling me. The husband shoved me out of a top floor window."

"Jesus."

"Yeah. I'm inclined to think that they were part of the cult themselves, though what scheme they were trying to pull with all their talk about the wife's sister is beyond me."

"Well, it looks like they got theirs along with the rest of them," said Sheriff Cole. "It's going to take some time to ID all these bodies. Dental records for most of them, I figure. I just wish we knew what the hell happened here."

"More evidence might turn up," said Garrett, "but it wouldn't surprise me if we won't be able to piece it together. These people, whoever they were, were keen to keep in the shadows and were pretty good at covering their tracks."

"Yeah. Just one of those things that comes along every once in a while that doesn't seem to have any rhyme or reason to it."

"Eerie."

"Yeah. Real eerie."

At a truck stop just outside of Victorville, Grant Calsom stuffed the last of his ham on rye sandwich into his mouth and washed it down with the dregs of his coffee cup. The headlights of trucks and cars flashed passed the windows of the diner. It was late and he still had a ways to go. He paid his bill and got up to leave.

The diner was busy for this time of night. Most of the booths were occupied by truckers but there was a woman cradling a baby in the booth by the door. The waitress was giving her a baby bottle of milk that she had warmed up in the kitchen.

"Thank you," said the woman. "I'm so sorry, I don't have any money to pay you with ..."

"That's alright honey," the waitress replied. "We can spare a little milk. But you can't stay here all night."

"Oh, I'm sure I can find somebody here who'll give me a ride," the woman replied.

The waitress bit her lip. "Are you sure there isn't somebody you can call? It's not right a woman and her babe travelling the roads at night. Don't you have any family?"

"No," the woman replied. "I have nobody."

The waitress left her and as she passed Grant she put a hand on his chest. "Say, Grant," she said.

"What's up, Anne?"

"Do you think you could give that poor woman a ride?"

Grant looked at the woman who was feeding her babe from the bottle and frowned. "Where's she headed?"

"She doesn't seem to know. Or care. I think she's on the run from a wifebeater. Leastways she has nothing on her, no money, no clothes, no baby gear. She's in a real spot, Grant."

"All right, all right," Grant said. "I'll talk to her."

"You're a sweetie."

Grant nodded with world-weary acceptance and headed over to the woman.

"I hear you're in need of a ride," he said.

"Yes, I am," the woman replied. "I'd be very grateful."

"I'm headed for Las Vegas. That in the right direction for you?"

"That's fine."

He frowned. "If you don't mind my saying, Lady, you don't seem to care where you're headed."

"Oh, anywhere is fine," she replied. "As long as it's away from here."

"You running from something?"

"Something like that."

"All right, I won't ask any more questions. You ready to go?"

"Sure."

She got up and the baby gurgled softly in her arms. Grant held open the door for her and they walked across the asphalt towards his big rig. He helped her up into the cab and then went around to clamber up into the driver's seat. With a roar of the engine, they rolled out of the truck stop and onto the highway.

The baby made soft, happy noises and the woman cooed to it. "He seems to like the rumble of the truck," she explained to Grant.

Grant glanced over at the baby. He saw its small, dark eyes fixed on him, examining him thoroughly. He was happy to help a poor single mother out but for some reason, and he didn't know why, that baby's eyes gave him a sense of great unease.

He tore his eyes from the baby's gaze and focused them on the road ahead as the truck sailed on into the night.

www.ingramcontent.com/pod-product-compliance
Lightning Source LLC
Chambersburg PA
CBHW050919220726
PP18604600001B/20